"Brilliant . . . Compelling . . .
One of the Recognized Masters
of Science Fiction."
—James Gunn, author of *The Mind Master*

"Terrific . . . . Aldiss does a convincing job creating his island, with all its dangerous corners and mysterious inhabitants."
—*The New York Times*

"A fast-paced, suspenseful adventure story."
—*Library Journal*

"A timely variation on the timeless concerns of *Doctor Moreau*."
—*Washington Post Book World*

"Aldiss at his best . . . . Disturbing for its relevance to contemporary science and scientific ethics."
—*Denver Post*

AN ISLAND CALLED MOREAU

Brian W. Aldiss

A TIMESCAPE BOOK

PUBLISHED BY POCKET BOOKS NEW YORK

A Timescape Book published by
POCKET BOOKS, a Simon & Schuster division of
GULF & WESTERN CORPORATION
1230 Avenue of the Americas, New York, N.Y. 10020

ISBN: 0-671-83533-5

First Timescape Books printing December, 1981

10 9 8 7 6 5 4 3 2 1

POCKET and colophon are trademarks of Simon & Schuster.

Use of the TIMESCAPE trademark is by exclusive
license from Gregory Benford, the trademark owner.

Also available in Simon and Schuster trade edition.

Printed in the U.S.A.

*Dedicated to the spirit
of H. G. Wells: The Master*

Contents

AN ISLAND
CALLED
MOREAU

To sink below the surface of the ocean was to enter a world of sound. Much of the sound originated from organic beings, forever transmitting their signals and necessities in harmonics which ranged through a scale commensurate with their environment, from shrillest, fastest squeak to deepest grunt. No one ear in that great element could encompass the span of frequencies involved.

Near the surface of the ocean, the sounds were light and many, and the organisms transmitting them similarly multitudinous and small. Lower, where larger fish swam, a deeper note prevailed. Lower still, deeper yet. As the light faded, as pressure increased toward the submerged valleys and hills of the ocean bed, the sounds became infrequent and acquired a lugubrious note in keeping with their surroundings.

Another range of sounds also persisted. It issued from another order of existence entirely: from the inorganic, from the mantle of water which moved ceaselessly over the drowned landscapes of its domain. These throatless noises had been audible almost since the beginning of time, certainly long before any stirrings of life. Currents, waves, tides, sunken rivers, sunken lakes and seas, all served as restless atmosphere to a world remote from the sentient creatures whose existences were confined to exposed territories outcropping above the planetary waters.

This ocean was of considerable depth. Its dimensions extended for thousands of miles in all directions. It occupied one-third of the surface of the planet, covering an area greater than that of all the exposed lands. A philosophical observer might regard it as the subconscious of the world, contrasting it to the exposed land area, which might—in the light of this rather whimsical notion—be considered as the seat of a fitful conscious.

In the aqueous subconscious of the planet, all was as usual, all as it had been for millions of years. On land, away in another element, the teeming individual awarenesses of the dominant species were in more than normal ferment. Their actions were full of sound and fury. They had just launched themselves into a global war which threatened to lay waste much of the land area, besides bringing about their own extinction.

Such military clamor scarcely penetrated the surface of the great ocean. Yet even there—even there, one could search and find contraindications, symptoms of pain.

Meteorites flashing through the night sky from space were once regarded as portents of solemn events. The ocean also had its portents from an alien element. Like a shower of meteoritic debris, metal from a disintegrating craft scattered across miles of sea. Slowly the parts sank, turning through the water, reflecting less and less light from above as they fell. They drifted down toward areas of enormous pressure and permanent twilight.

Finally, all that remained of the Leda came to rest upon a barren plain near the equator, bedding down in primordial oozes under six thousand meters of ocean.

1

Alone in the Pacific

In times of peace, the crashing of the space shuttle *Leda* into the Pacific Ocean would have provided drama enough for most of the world to have heard about it by lunchtime. During the early months of war in 1996, the incident was little noticed, beyond the announcement that an Undersecretary of State was missing.

It is not my intention to detail that crash here. It forms no part of the dreadful story I have to relate. Suffice it to say that my secretary and I were the only passengers, and that the crew numbered two, James Fan Toy and Jose Galveston. The shuttle splashed down into the Pacific close to the equator, latitude 2° south, longitude 178° east. My secretary was killed on impact; in a moment of panic, he jumped up just before we struck, and his neck was broken.

The craft floated long enough for Fan Toy, Galveston, and me to climb free and jump into an inflatable life raft.

To escape drowning was one thing, to escape the ocean another. The war was far away to the north of us, and we were in a little-frequented sector of ocean. We saw no planes, no ships, no land. Day succeeded day, the awful power of the sun making itself continually felt. We had little shelter and less water, rationing ourselves to a mouthful twice a day. As our life energies were burned from us, we took to lying under an inflatable plastic canopy, no longer paddling or even keeping watch on the unvarying horizon about us.

On the eighth day, early in the morning before the sun had risen high enough to scorch us, Fan Toy gave a cry and pointed to something floating in the waves. We stood and stared, leaning against each other for support.

How vividly I recall that moment, with the stench of our bodies and the boat's fabric, the ceaseless motion of the waves, the vast expanse of water! In the water was a dolphin, making slowly toward us.

"It's bringing help," Fan Toy said. We had sent out a radio call for help as the *Leda* reentered Earth's atmosphere. This might well be a naval dolphin coming to guide us to a nearby submarine—such was the hope raised by sight of the creature.

"Don't be too sure he's on our side," Galveston said.

We dipped our hands into the ocean and splashed our blistered faces and eye sockets to try and see more clearly.

"Yes, it's one of our boys," Fan Toy said. "Take a look at the stars and stripes embedded in its tail."

I was peering too and could discern the insignia as he spoke.

"It's moving slowly. Could be it's injured," I said.

The creature seemed to be making heavy weather of what was just a light swell; it wallowed from side to side as it headed toward us.

Galveston got a paddle out. "I don't like the look of the beast. Keep off!" He struck at the dolphin as it came within range.

"Don't be a fool," Fan Toy said, trying to knock the paddle from Galveston's hand. The two men struggled feebly together.

My attention was momentarily attracted elsewhere. A school of flying fish—only the second school we had seen since taking to the life raft—passed behind us, clipping the waves as it flew. One of them, slightly adrift from its fellows, landed in the raft behind us.

It was food. As I stooped down to seize it, my glance caught something on the far horizon. I could not say what it was—possibly the mast of a ship, gleaming in the sun. I bent down to snatch at the struggling fish.

As well that I did. In that moment came the explosion. It

struck me with a wall of sound and pitched me into the sea.

I surfaced, choking and deafened. The water seethed all round me. The life raft had gone. So had Fan Toy and Galveston. I called their names. Limbs and flesh lay in the ocean about me, trailing tentacles of red which were dispersed among the waters. They had been blown apart, as had dolphin and raft.

The one item still afloat and happily intact was the inflatable canopy. I managed to climb into it, bail out the water with my hands, and achieve a precarious stability. I also managed to retrieve a paddle. Then I lay where I was, in a daze, as slowly my hearing returned: but not my companions.

For whatever reason, I had again been preserved. Triumphantly, I told myself—even whispered the words aloud through cracked lips—that my love of God and country would bring me through all perils to victory. I did not doubt that the *Leda* had been sabotaged by subversive elements in the Moon base, and that the sabotage had been aimed at me. Yet I had survived. And would continue to survive.

Maybe Fan Toy and Galveston had been involved in the treachery, for one can trust no one during a global war. They had been destroyed. I lived.

Now I had a makeshift boat. I was too numb at first to paddle. But a light breeze caught the canopy and bore me along, slowly increasing the distance between me and the carnage. Which was as well. Two sharks began to circle the area. Then another moved in, and another after. Soon I watched many triangular fins, circling the bloodied area at speed.

There was little doubt as to what had occurred. The dolphin had been naval trained. It must have been on a suicide mission, loaded with an explosive charge, maybe a nuclear one, and programmed for some particular target. Enemy defenses had hit and wounded it. Half senseless, it had swum on, who knew how far. Seeing our raft, it had homed in on us, probably in search of aid. Galveston had struck it with his paddle, whereupon the explosive charge had been detonated.

Confirmation of this theory lay in the way we found the dolphin swimming alone. An ordinary dolphin, when wounded, secures help from its own kind, who will escort it hundreds of miles, if need be, to a safe spot where it can recuperate. Our fellow, loaded with death, had had to travel alone to the last.

It was impossible to stand in my flimsy canopy boat. I could manage only to sit up and stare about me, searching the horizon for that gleaming thing again. It was nowhere in sight.

My strength began to desert me as hope went. The sun was growing powerful, and I crammed a flexible bucket on my head for protection. Then I slumped back as best I could, unable to paddle since there was nowhere to paddle to.

Seconds, minutes, hours, drifted by before I looked up again. Who knows the teeming thoughts that poured through my mind? When I finally broke from my reverie and peered about me, an island was in sight!

How beautiful it looked, how superbly more positive, more *created,* than the miserable element swilling all about me! I stood up in my excitement and capsized my boat immediately. Once I was back in it again, I turned eagerly to see what I could see.

At this distance, the land appeared as a rock with a flat top. On that top, an installation of some kind had been built; this was what I had seen as I stooped to pick up the flying fish. Although any indication of human enterprise filled me with hope, I had reservations from the beginning; the world was so full of automated machinery of various kinds, from missile detection systems to navigational aids, that evidence of an installation was no proof men would be nearby. Yet even a deserted island was a hundred times more welcome than open sea. To die under a palm tree suddenly seemed like heaven.

The island was still distant. A current was carrying me toward it, and I was content for a while to lie back in exhaustion and be borne onward. Again my mind wandered, half deliriously; I became involved in complex situations with people I did not know but thought I recognized.

When I shook myself from my lethargy, the sun was low in the west and magnificent layers of cloud were drawing about it to celebrate its descent. The island was considerably nearer; I could make out gray walls of cliff. The installation was lost in late afternoon light.

My drinking water was entirely gone. Exhausted though I was, I seized on the paddle and tried to guide my frail craft toward the island. For a dread filled me that ocean currents might carry me past this refuge in the hours of darkness, and that by morning it would lie far astern. Then I should surely die. My chance was now—or never again.

I was still paddling as night came down. It was glorious and terrible to witness the world's swift change from day to night; even in my drained condition, I was moved by it, and offered a prayer to God.

The breeze which had earlier carried me westward was reversed with evening. My boat was almost at a standstill. I battled in the darkness as long as I could, collapsing at last in the bottom of my craft, where I slept fitfully, half in a delirium.

I woke before dawn, chilled all through, convinced I was dying. I lay like a broken bundle, cradling my paddle, with my jaw hanging open and my mouth parched, as once more the processes of Earth brought this part of the world into light.

I opened my eyes and lifted my head. Great cliffs loomed close, lit by early sun. They rose steeply from the waves without a shore. High above the waterline bushes grew, crowning the cliffs. Birds wheeled above them. I stared at the birds in wonder. My canopy was moving slowly westward again, no more than three hundred meters from the cliffs.

One detail was especially remarkable. Carved into the cliff at a place which appeared totally inaccessible was a gigantic letter.

The letter dominated me. I stared at it, trying to make sense out of it, but to my dazed imagining it seemed to be independent of meaning, to exist only for itself. Its very shape suggested a sturdy bipedal independence. It was a huge letter **M**.

The cliffs dazzled with reflected light but the **M** was black. Whoever had sculpted it from the rock had made certain that it was visible from afar by filling its recesses with tar or some black pitchy substance.

Thoughts of vaguely religious nature filled my mind. I heard my voice from my cracked lips say, "In the beginning was the letter." I laughed feebly. Then I slumped back into the boat.

When I brought myself to look again, the **M** stood some way behind, a double black pillar. The nearer cliffs were less steep and in shadow. Trees were more in evidence. I even imagined I might have seen a building among the trees, as my head drooped once more. But the insistence that I should do something rose within me, and again I dragged myself up. I splashed head and neck with seawater, although the brine made my lips smart.

The boat was drifting past a southwest-facing cliff wall which lay no more than two hundred meters away. Ordinarily, I would have thought nothing of swimming ashore; now, all I could do was cup my hands and call for help; but there was the noise of surf against rocks to compete with, and my throat was choked by drought.

I could see that in less than an hour we should reach the end of the island, to be carried into the open ocean again. The cliffs were becoming less massive. It would be possible to scramble ashore at the westernmost point. When it came level, then I would have to fling myself into the water, trusting to God and the remainder of my strength to get me ashore.

As I was preparing for this ordeal, I discovered that I was being observed. Three or four natives stood under tall trees among bushes, watching me. At this distance, I could get no clear view, yet something about them—whether in their faces or their stances—gave an impression of singular bestiality. They stood almost immobile and stared across the waves at me; then they were gone; the bushes moved for a moment and were still.

I turned my attention to the end of the island, which could now be seen to sprout an islet just beyond its shores, leaving a narrow channel between shore and islet. The question seemed to be, whether the current which carried me would sweep me clear away from the island or closely round its tip, between island and islet; if the latter was the case, it should not be impossible to get ashore.

As I considered this question, a heavy craft with thundering engine swerved out from behind the island. Spreading a wake of white water behind it, it curved out and headed toward me.

Two men were in the craft. I could get clear glimpses only of the man at the wheel. His face was black and again, as with the watchers on the cliff, I received an impression of brutishness.

The craft he steered was painted a muddy brown. As it bore toward me and swung clumsily abeam, the wash from it swamped my canopy. I found myself struggling in the water. Half drowned, I heard the curses of the men in the boat; then my wrists were grasped, and my shoulders, and I was heaved unceremoniously into the landing craft, as it was referred to.

As soon as they had me on deck, the boat was in motion again, swerving violently about. I was left to roll on the deck like a freshly landed tunny, coughing and spewing the sea-water out of me.

When I had recovered slightly, I heaved myself into a sitting position. I was confronted by as frightful a counte-nance as I have ever seen in my life. At close quarters, its brutishness was overwhelming, so that I half believed I was delirious.

Under a floppy leather hat was no brow, simply a great swelling face covered with stubble. The jaw was prognath-ous with no chin. A mighty mouth swept back, its corners almost vanishing into the absurd hat, its fleshy lips hardly fleshy enough to conceal large incisors in the lower jaw. Above this formidable mouth was a snout-like nose, wrin-kled in a sneer like a hyena's, and two almost lidless eyes. These eyes regarded me now—fixed themselves on me with a dull red glare. I pulled myself back from them in shock. But still I had to stare into them.

The monster regarded me with the strangest expression, at once aggressive and shrinking, as though it was on the point of either throwing itself upon me or leaping out of my way.

Only for a moment did we stare at each other so closely. Only for a moment was that strange ambiguity of gaze be-tween us. Then the black man was struck on the back by his companion, who roared, "Get to the helm, George! None of your tricks!"

Black George leaped back to his station with a frantic scuffle, quite devoid of dignity. He was a big burly fellow, with tremendous shoulders on him, but short in the shank. He was encased in an all-enveloping pair of gray work over-alls.

When I turned my attention to the other man, my first impressions were scarcely more favorable. A fine place I had come to! I thought. This specimen was recognizably Caucasian, and with no visible deformities, but he was also a great hulking brute. His face was fat and pasty; it bore a besotted, sullen expression. His eyes seemed to be the same pasty color as his skin; they looked directly into mine once, for an instant, then away, in such a furtive manner that I was as disconcerted as by George's savage stare. He always avoided a direct gaze.

Although everything about him appeared totally unfavorable—apart from the cardinal fact that he had rescued me from the sea—I gained an impression that he was an intelligent, even sensitive, man who was trying to bury some dreadful knowledge within him: and that the effort had brutalized him.

His hair was tawny and uncared for and he had a straggling yellowy-brown beard. He carried a military carbine slung over one shoulder and clutched a bottle in his left hand.

When he saw me regarding him, he held out the bottle before him, not looking straight at me, and said mockingly, "You look as if you could have use for a drink, hero!"

I said, "I need water."

My voice was a croak. His was thick and had a curious accent. It took a while before I realized English was not his native language.

"Palm wine for the morning. Fresh vintage. Do you plenty good!"

"I need water."

"Suit yourself. You must wait till we are on the shore."

George was now swinging the craft in between island and terminal islet, hunched with a kind of careful ferocity over the wheel. I could see a strip of beach beyond. The blond man yelled to George to go more steadily.

"What is this place?" I asked.

He looked me over again, half between pity and contempt, his eyes sliding round me.

"Welcome to Moreau Island, hero," he said. He took another swig at his bottle.

2

Some Company Ashore

The landing craft ran into a narrow channel with rock on the left and island on the right. Open sea ahead indicated that although the island was several kilometers long, it was considerably less in width, at least at this western end. The beach was a slender strip of sand, bracketed in rocks and stones and encroached by scrub. George brought us swinging broadside on to this strip, hunching himself by the wheel and awaiting further instructions while he eyed me with distrust.

"Are you fit enough to walk?" the blond man asked me.

"I can try," I said.

"You're going to have to try, hero. This is where you get out! No ambulances here. I've got the fishing nets to see to, and that's trouble enough to do. George here will take you along to HQ. Get that?"

Involuntarily, I looked at George with suspicion.

"He won't hurt you," the blond man said. "If you drifted through the minefields okay, then you will be safe by George."

"What sort of a place am I getting to? Are there other— white men here? I don't even know your name."

The blond man looked down at the deck and rubbed his soiled deck shoes against each other.

"You aren't welcome here, hero, you ought better to face that fact. Moreau Island is not geared exactly to cater to the tourist trade. But we can maybe find a use for you."

"My work is elsewhere," I said sharply. "A lot of people will be looking for me right now. The ASASC shuttle I was in crashed in the Pacific some way from here. My name is Calvert Roberts, and I hold down an important governmental post. What's your name? You still haven't told me."

"It's not any damned business of yours, is it? My name is Hans Maastricht and I'm not ashamed of it. Now, get on shore. I have work to do or I will be into trouble."

He turned to George, slapping the carbine over his shoulder to emphasize his words. "You take this man straight to HQ, get that? You go with him to Master. You no stop on the way, you no cause any trouble. Okay? You no let other People cause any trouble, savvy?"

George looked at him, then at me, then back to the other man, swinging his head in a confused way.

"Does he speak English?" I asked.

"This is what he savvies best," Maastricht said, slapping the carbine again. "Hurry it up, George. Help this man to HQ. I'll be back when I've checked the fishing nets."

"Savvy," said George. "Hurry it up. Help this man HQ, come back when I check the nets."

"You just get him safe to HQ," Maastricht said, clouting him across the shoulders.

The hulking fellow jumped down into shallow water and put out a hand to help me. I say "hand"—it was a black leathery deformed thing he extended to me. There was nothing to do but take it. I had to jump down and fell practically into his arms, leaning for a moment against his barrel chest. Again I felt in him the same revulsion as struggled in myself. He moved back one pace in one hop, catching me off balance, so that I fell on my hands and knees in the shallow waters.

"Sort yourselves out!" Maastricht shouted, with a laugh. Swinging the carbine round on its sling, he fired one shot in the air, presumably as a warning, then headed the landing craft toward where the channel widened.

George watched him go, then turned to me almost timorously. His gaze probed mine; being almost neckless, he hunched his shoulders to do so, as if he were shortsighted.

At the same time, he extended that maimed hand to me. I was still on my knees in the water. There was something poignant in the fellow's gesture. I took his arm and drew myself up.

"Thank you, George."

"Me George. You no call George?"

"My name is Calvert Roberts. I'm glad of your help."

"You got Four Limbs Long. You glad of your help." He put his paw to his head as if trying to cope with concepts beyond his ability. "You glad me help. You glad George help."

"Yes. I'm feeling kind of shaky."

He gestured toward the open water. "You—find in water, yes?"

It was as if he were striving to visualize something that had happened long ago.

"Which way to your HQ, George?"

"HQ, yes, we go, no trouble. No stop on way, no cause any trouble." His voice held a curious clotted quality. We stood on the stony beach, with a fringe of palm trees and scrub to landward, while a comedy of misdirected intentions developed—or it might have been a comedy if I had had the strength to find the situation funny. George did not know whether he should walk before me or behind me or beside me. His shuffling movements suggested that he was reluctant to adopt any of the alternatives.

The surface amiability of our conversation (if it can be dignified by that word) in no way calmed my fear of George. He was monstrous, and his close physical presence remained abhorrent. Something in his posture inspired distrust. That jackal sneer on his face seemed at war all the time with a boarish element in his composition, so that I was in permanent doubt as to whether he was going to turn round and run away or to charge at me; and a certain nervous shuffle in his step kept that doubt uppermost in my mind.

"You lead, I'll follow, George."

I thought he was about to dash away into the bushes. I tried again.

"All right. I'll go ahead and you can follow me."

I thought he was about to rush at me.

"You no drive me?"

"I want to get to HQ, George. I must have water. There's no danger, is there?"

He shook his great head to and fro, saying, "Danger, yes.

No. No stop on way, no cause any trouble. Go with him to Master.''

I began to walk. He darted forward immediately and remained exactly one pace behind, his little piggy eyes glaring into mine whenever I turned my head. Had I not felt so exhausted, I should have been more frightened or more amused than I was.

In my condition and in this company, I was not well equipped to appreciate scenery. It presented, however, an immediate solid impression to me, an impression formidable and silent. Underfoot was that broken marginal territory which marks the division between ocean and land, even so precarious a wedge of land as this. Just ahead were bleached rocks and the somber greens of palm and thorn bushes. The ocean was at its eternal stir; the foliage hung silent and waiting, and far from welcoming.

The undergrowth came down close to the water's edge. I saw a track leading among the trees, and took it.

George had evidently summed me up by now; for he said, ''He got Four Limbs Long. You got Four Limbs Long.''

''That's how it happens to be with mankind,'' I said sharply.

George said, or rather chanted, '' 'Four Limbs Long—Wrong Kind of Song!' ''

''Where did you get that idea from?'' I asked. But I did not stand and wait for his answer. I set off along the path, and he sprang to follow on my heels, one pace behind. It was a relief to be among trees again, in shade. After all the days in the boat, my walk was uncertain, although I felt strength returning as we proceeded.

My mind was preoccupied with many things, not least with my weakness and the contrasting strength of the moronic brute behind me. I was also puzzled by what Maastricht—whom I took for a Netherlander from his name and his accent—had said: ''Welcome to Moreau Island.'' The name meant something to me, yet I could not place it at all. Moreau Island? Had some scandal been connected with it?

Despite these preoccupations, I took care to keep alert to my surroundings, for there had been something threatening in Maastricht's warning to George. What or whom were we likely to meet?

This strip of the island had little to offer, apart from the singular virtue of being terra firma. The rock to our right hand, sculptured as if by water at some earlier period of history, harbored many scuttling things, though probably nothing more exotic than birds and lizards. Bamboos were all about us, growing from cavities in the rock and from the ground, which was littered with stones and large shells. They grew thickly enough to obstruct our passage, though thinly enough for a pattern of sunlight and shadow to be cast where we walked. Occasionally we caught glimpses of the bright sea to our left, through a trellis of leaves.

At one point, I almost tripped over one of the large shells. Kicking it aside, I observed that it was the whitened and empty shell of a tortoise. We seemed almost to be walking through a tortoise graveyard, so thick did the shells lie; there was never a sign of a live one.

Boulders lay close on either side, some of them as tall as we were. Then we had to thread our way between them, and George came uncomfortably close to my vulnerable neck. Two of these big boulders virtually formed a gateway; beyond them, more of George's uncouth breed of native were lurking.

I saw them among the thickets ahead and halted despite myself.

Turning to George, I said, "Why are they in hiding? What's the matter with them?"

With a crafty look, at once furtive and menacing, George said, " 'Four Limbs Long—Wrong Kind of Song. . . . Four Limbs Short—Right Kind of Sport!' " His feet began a kind of shuffle in the dust. His eyes would not meet mine.

There was no point in trying to make conversation with him. Now that his own kind were close, he looked more dangerous than ever.

"George, you take me straight to HQ, savvy? You no stop, you no cause trouble, you no let anybody cause trouble, okay? You savvy?"

He began to pant in a doggy way, his tongue hanging out. "You no got carbine, Cal—" Perhaps he struggled to recall my surname; if so he failed, and his use of my given name carried an unwelcome familiarity.

I was remembering what Maastricht had said, "*Master got carbine!*"

He moved one burly shoulder at me, looking away, mumbling, "Yes, savvy *Master* got carbine . . ."

"Come on, then!" Advancing between the boulders, I called, "Stand back ahead. We are in a hurry."

An amazing array of faces peered out of the bushes. They

bore a family resemblance to George, although there was
great variety in their deformity. Here were snouts that
turned up and proboscises that turned down; mouths with
no lips, mouths with serrated lips; hairless faces and faces
covered almost completely with hair or stubble; eyes that
glared with no visible lids, eyes that dreamed under heavy
lids like horses'. All these faces were turned suspiciously
toward me, noses twitching in my direction, and all managed
to avoid my direct gaze by a hairbreadth. From some eyes
in the deeper shadows, I caught the red or green blank glare
of iridescence, as if I were confronted by animals from a
ludicrous fairy tale.

Indeed, I recalled series of drawings by artists like Charles
Le Brun and Thomas Rowlandson, in which the physiognomies of men and women merged through several transfor-
mations into the physiognomies of animals—bulls, lions,
leopards, dogs, oxen, and pigs. The effect was absurd as
well as alarming. I moved forward, clapping my hands
slowly, and slowly they gave way.

But they were calling to George, who still followed me.

"Has he not Four Limbs Long?"

"Is he from the Lab'raty?"

"Where is the one with the bottle?"

"Has he a carbine?"

And other things I could not understand, for I was soon to
learn that George's diction was a marvel of distinctness
among his friends, and he a creature of genius among mo-
rons. He still followed stubbornly behind me, saying, or
rather chanting—most of their sentences were in singsong
—"He find in big water. He Four Limbs Long. He Five
Fingers Long—Not Wise or Strong. No stop, no cause trouble. Plenty beat at HQ."

He chanted. I staggered beside him. They fell back or
hopped back, letting us through—but hands with maimed
stubs of fingers, hands more like paws or hooves, reached
out and touched me as I went by.

Now I caught a strong rank smell, like the whiff of a tiger
cage in a zoo. The trees and bushes thinned, the sun beat
down more strongly, and we came to the native village.

Near the first houses, a rock on my right hand rose in a
high wall. Climbers and vines, some brilliantly flowering,
hung down the rock face, and among them fell a slender
waterfall, splashing from shelf to shelf of the rock. It filled a
small pool, where it had been muddied and fouled. But I ran

to the rock, and let the blessed stuff fall direct onto my face, my lips, my parched tongue, my throat! Ah, that moment! In truth, the waterfall was not much more than a drip, but Niagara itself could not have been more welcome!

After a while, I had to rest dizzily against the rock, letting the water patter on the back of my neck. I could hear the natives stealthily gather about me. But I offered a prayer of thanks for my deliverance before I turned to face them.

Their ungainly bodies were hidden under the same coveralls that George wore; many an unseemly bulk was thus concealed from the world. One or two of them wore boots; most went barefoot. Some had made barbaric attempts to decorate themselves with shells or bits of bone in their hair or round their necks. Only later did I realize that these were the females of this wonderfully miscegenous tribe.

Fascinated as I was with them, I believe they were far more fascinated with me.

"He laps water," one said, sidling up and addressing me without meeting my gaze.

"I drink water, as I guess you must," I said. I was torn between curiosity and apprehension, not knowing whether to try to establish communication or make a break for it, but at least this creature who came forward looked as harmless as any of them. George resembled an outré blend of boar and hyena; this creature looked like a kind of dog. He had the fawning aspect of a mongrel which one sometimes notices in human beings even in more favored parts of the world.

"What's your name?" I asked, pointing at him to get the message home.

He slunk back a pace. " 'The Master's is the Hand that Maims. The Master's is the Voice that Names. . . .' "

"What is your name?"

He touched his pouting chest humbly. "Your name Bernie. Good man, good boy."

"Yes, you're a good man, Bernie." Weakness and a touch of hysteria overcame me. To find a Bernie here in this miserable patch of jungle on some forgotten rock in the Pacific —a Bernie looking so much like a stray pooch—was suddenly funny. Why, I thought, Bernie as in Saint Bernard! I began helplessly to laugh, collapsing against the rock. I still laughed when I found myself sitting in the mud. When they clustered nearer to me, staring down in a bovine way, I covered my face and laughed and wept.

I scarcely heard the whistle blow.

They heard. "The Master Knows! The Master Blows!" They milled about uneasily. I looked up, afraid of being trampled on. Then one started to run and they all followed, stampeding as if they were a herd of cattle. George stood till last, looking at me with a great puzzlement from under his hat, muttering to himself. Then he too attempted to flee.

He was too late. The Master appeared. George sank to the ground, covering his head with humble slavish gesture. A whip cracked across his shoulders and then the Master passed him and strode toward me.

Climbing slowly to my feet, I stood with my back to the rock. I was tempted to imitate the natives and take to my heels.

The so-called Master was tremendously tall! I reckoned he was at least three meters high, impossibly tall for a human being.

I could see him among the trees and huts, marching along a wide track, and not much more than fifty meters from me. I had a glimpse of tranquil waters behind him, but all my attention was concentrated on him.

He carried a carbine in the alert position, ready to fire. It was aimed at me in a negligent sort of way. His stride was one of immeasurable confidence; there was about it something rigid and mechanical.

His face was concealed beneath a helmet. I could not see his eyes. As he came near, I saw that his arms and legs were of metal and plastic.

"My God, it's a robot!" I said aloud.

Then it came round the corner of the rock and confronted me.

"Where did you spring from?" it demanded.

3

In the Hands
of the Master

One of my reasons for believing in God has been the presence in my life of emotions and understandings not susceptible to scientific method. I have met otherwise scientific men who believe in telepathy while denying God. To me, it makes more sense to believe in God than telepathy; telepathy seems to me to be unscientific mumbo-jumbo like astrology (although I have met men working prosaically on the Moon who held an unshakable belief in astrology), while God can never be unscientific, because he is the Prime Mover who contains science along with all the other effects of our universe. Or so I had worked it out, to my temporary satisfaction. God's shifting ground.

Directly I faced the Master, I felt some of those emotions —call them empathic if you will—which I have referred to as being unsusceptible to scientific method. Directly he spoke, I knew that in him, as in his creatures, aggression and fear were mixed. God gave me understanding.

This could not be a robot.

I looked up at him. Once I got a grip on myself, I saw that the Master, although indeed a fearsome figure, was not as tall as I had estimated in my near panic. He stood perhaps two and a quarter meters high, which is to say just over a head taller than I.

Beneath his helmet was a pale face which sweated just like mine did.

"Who are you, and where did you spring from?" he demanded.

I am trained to understand men, to cut through their poses. I understand tough men, and men who have merely tough facades. Despite the truculence of this man's voice, I thought I detected uncertainty in it. I moved forward from the rock where I had been leaning.

He shuffled awkwardly in order to remain facing me, at the same time swinging his gun up to aim it at my stomach. Once my attention was thus directed to it, I recognized the riot gun as a kind issued to Co-Allied Invasion and Occupation Forces. It was a Xiay 25A, cheaply manufactured by our Chinese allies, capable of multiple-role usage, firing ordinary bullets, CS gas bullets, nail bombs, and other similar devices. The robot-like man carried a whip and a revolver in his belt. He was well armed if he was out for a morning walk.

He repeated his question.

I faced him squarely, fighting down my weakness.

"I'm American, which I believe is more than you can claim. My name is Calvert Madle Roberts, and I am an Undersecretary of State in the Willson Administration. I was returning from state business when my plane was shot down in the Pacific. Your employees brought me ashore. I have to get in touch with Washington immediately."

"My employees? You must mean Maastricht. What the devil was he playing at, landing you here? This isn't a funfair I'm running. A carnival, you'd say, being American. Why didn't he bring you round to the lagoon?"

"I've been nine days adrift. I'm about all in and I need to contact my department soonest, okay? If you're in charge, I hold you responsible for looking after me."

He uttered a grunt which might have represented laughter. "I am in charge here, that's for sure. . . . And I can't very well have you thrown back into the ocean."

"That's big of you. I've told you my name. Roberts. What's your name?"

His lip curled slightly. "You call me Master, same as the rest of them do." He swung himself about with a violent

bodily motion and began striding back the way he had come.
I followed.

We made our way along what served as a wretched street
for the native village. The natives, having gathered their
courage, had returned to peer at us. They uttered apotropaic
phrases as their Master went by.

"His is the Hand that Maims. . . .
"His is the Head that Blames. . . .
"His is the Whip that Tames. . . ."

Beyond the little ragged village lay the lagoon. The road
skirted it, winding past its tranquil green waters to buildings
glimpsed through trees. Beyond everything was a steep hill,
its gray cliffs looming above the jungle. However mean the
affairs of men, Nature had added a note of grandeur.

It was impossible to keep up with the great mechanical
strides of the self-styled Master. I lagged farther and farther
behind. There was a gang of natives working on the far side
of the lagoon, where I observed a mobile crane; they stopped
work to stare at us.

My vision began to waver as I moved uphill. A stockade
of tall and rusty metal posts stood here. The top of the stockade was decorated with barbed wire, strand after entangled
strand of it. The Master halted at a narrow gate in the wall,
stooping awkwardly to unlock it. I heard tumblers click
back. He turned a wheel, the gate swung open, and he
passed in. As soon as I had followed him, he pushed the gate
shut and locked it from the inside.

Weakness overcame me. I fell to one knee.

"Bella!" he called, ignoring me.

I rose again, making my way forward as a strange figure
came out of a building toward us. It was wearing a dress. It
—no, she, Bella, had the short deformed legs common to
most of the other islanders. Her skin was a dull pink. Her
face was as hideous as George's and his fellows', although
her eyes were curiously—lambent, I believe the word is.
They seemed to glow and had an oriental cast. She would
not look directly at me, although she approached readily
enough while listening to what the Master was telling her.

To my surprise, she came straight up to me and attempted
to lift me off my feet. I felt a sort of nervous thrill at her
embrace. Then I collapsed.

My senses never entirely left me. I was aware of strange
faces about me, and of being carried into a shadowy room.
Something cool was placed on my forehead. Water was

poured into my mouth; I could hardly swallow, and the cup was taken away. Then my eyes were bandaged. I lay without volition as expert hands ran over my body and I was given a thorough examination. These were things that hardly registered at the time, although they came back to me afterward.

When I finally roused, the bandage was off my eyes. I lay naked under a sheet and felt refreshed. As I propped myself up on one elbow, I saw that an ointment to soothe my sunburns had been applied to my chest and face. The woman called Bella sat hunched in one corner of the room. Her eyes flashed greenly at me as she turned her head.

"You—feel okay now?"

"I think so."

"You like whisky?"

"Thanks, but I don't drink."

"No drink? You drink water."

"I meant that I don't drink whisky."

She stared motionlessly at me. She had short dark hair. I wondered if it was a wig. She had a nose that resembled a cat's muzzle.

"Thanks for seeing me through, Bella. I was in a bad way. Just reaction."

"I tell Master." She slunk away, hardly opening the door enough to get through, closing it directly she was through it. Decidedly feline.

The room took on new proportions as soon as she had gone. My body felt extremely light. Well, I said to myself, that's how it is, here on the Moon. You mustn't expect reality. Reality here is only one-sixth of what it is on Earth.

Without any sense of effort, I climbed out of bed and found it was easy to stand on my two feet if I stretched out my arms for balance. Being naked made things much easier. I floated over to my one unglazed window. No glass: but of course there were no minerals on the Moon.

"**M** for Moon," I told myself aloud.

There was music, played close by, music and the strong heat of a tropical day. The music was Haydn's, that composer who had come to dominate all the others, even Bach and Beethoven, in the last decade. I believed it was his Fifty-fourth Symphony being played. Haydn and heat . . .

By some trick of the mind, I remembered who Moreau was.

I was gazing out at an untidy courtyard. Cans of paint were stacked there, sheets of wood, and panels of metal.

Maastricht, still clutching his bottle, crossed my line of sight. I had forgotten he was on the Moon.

I heard the Master shouting at him. "Why the hell did you dump that politician where you did? It was asking for trouble —this is no fun-fair! Suppose George had—"

"I didn't bother to take him round to the harbor because I was in a haste to get to the fish nets, like you told me," Maastricht's voice replied. "I've had enough shouting at for one day. George brought him in safely, didn't he?"

"I had to go and rescue the man. They were about to tear him apart, just to put you in the picture."

"Pfhuh! I don't believe you. Anyway, what do we do with the guy now he's here?"

"You know he can't be allowed to stay. Hypothesize, man. Suppose he took it into his head to team up with Warren?"

"Jeez, don't mention Warren. . . . Let it ride a while, Master. It's time I had a drink."

There was more, but strange waves were radiating through my head, bringing darkness. I staggered back to the bed, tucked a hand under the pillow, and fell into a deep, troubled sleep. Over and over again, I was half roused by the terrors of my dreams, in which the recurrent motif was a gigantic letter **M**, black, carved sometimes from rock, sometimes from flesh. Occasionally I roused to find the woman Bella ministering to me, or clumsily mopping my brow.

Since I was on the Moon, things were pleasant that would otherwise have been unpleasant. In her cat-like fashion, Bella pressed herself against me. Her mouth, with its sharp incisors, lay against mine. I enjoy power, and the wielding of it; in any given situation, I will maneuver until I am in control; but with Bella against me, fawning yet predatory, I relished the weakness in which I floated. Things go like that on Luna.

At last a time came when I sat up and was absolutely clear in my head. My internal clocks told me I had been in fever for two or more days. Neatly pressed clothes lay by my bed. I climbed out and stood. My shanks looked thinner than before. I tested my balance, and a faint heaving still lingered, a phantom of the days adrift in the boat; but I took command of myself and had no trouble walking across to the window.

There lay Moreau Island, soaking in the unending daily dosage of sun, with the Pacific waiting as always on the horizon, a vat of energy. In the untidy courtyard, a bird swooped. All else was motionless. The Moon had set below my psychic horizon. I returned to the bed and sat down.

A while later, Bella slunk into the room.

"You—are better?" she asked.

I beckoned her closer. She stayed where she was, one hand on the door. Scrutinizing her, I reassembled the mixed feelings I had toward her during my fever. She wore an ankle-length drab gold dress. It was torn. The tear, and her general demeanor, conveyed an impression of wretchedness; yet there was in her regard, in her hunched shoulder, a defiance which I admired. By the same token, she was ugly enough; yet there was an animality about her which had made some kind of appeal to my more carnal instincts.

"I appreciate your attentions to me while I was sick, Bella," I said. "Now I have to work. Where's your shower? I sure can use a shower."

"The Master wish to speak to you." Maybe she understood, maybe not.

She led me down a short corridor and into another room. Music was playing—Haydn again. I had expected to see the Master towering over me, but he was not there. It was quite a pleasant room, but almost bare of furniture. There was a long window which gave a view over the top of the palisade —almost a seductive view, you might say, if it were not for the sinister nature of the surroundings.

I could see part of a placid lagoon, where the water was almost turquoise and sheltered from the blue Pacific beyond by a spine of land which almost enclosed it. On the curve of the lagoon was a harbor, with a battered landing stage and a boat moored to it. Tall palms leaned across to the water, overshadowing some huts. Behind them was jungle, climbing up a slope, the top of which was lost behind the building in which I stood.

It was such a typical tropical view that I wondered if I had seen it before, perhaps in some previous reincarnation. Then I recalled that this vista embodied one of the favorite early twentieth-century dreams of escape from civilization: the retreat in the South Seas, where the steamer came from Europe once a month and the girls wore grass skirts. And I reflected, as I turned away to observe the Master's room, that I had a great deal for which to be thankful. Like life itself.

On one wall was a 3V screen: I was looking into a vast and ornate chamber, part perhaps of some German palace, in which an orchestra was seated, giving of their best to the soul of Joseph Haydn. I recognized the channel instantly as World Third; it beamed music out from Munich twenty-four hours of every day, and was available by satellite anywhere, even on this remote spot on the ocean. They could pick it up in Moon Base too. One of the good things that the war had not yet put a stop to.

Then the Master's voice cut in over the music, the orchestra dimmed, and he said, "I'm coming in to speak to you, Roberts. Are you prepared?"

"Certainly. What now?"

"You may be surprised."

At that, a side door opened, and someone entered from the next room. Maastricht followed, but I scarcely noticed him.

I was too busy looking at the first person who had entered.

It was the Master. I recognized the pallid face. He was about thirty-five years old. He was cut down to size since I last saw him swaggering along. He came rapidly forward in a mechanized wheelchair and halted in front of me. I backed away and sat down on a relaxer. He had no legs. A loose-flowing garment covered his body.

"This is where it's at, Mr. Roberts. Now you see me like this, we both know where we stand." He was full of old-fashioned slangy phrases from some decades back, and used this one without a hint of humor. "In any event, I can't take prosthetic limbs for very long in this heat. Now, you and I are going to have a little talk while Bella brings you in something to eat."

Peeled from his armor, and decked out in that loose-flowing garment, the self-styled Master looked weak and female on first impression. But in the pallid face with its sheer cheeks and narrow pale mouth I saw a remorseless quality that would have to be taken into account: either respected or circumvented.

As he turned to say something to the Netherlander who hovered by, I was busy estimating him.

"Tough luck about your accident," I said, indicating the elaborate wheelchair. "How come you're living on an island in the Pacific War Zone? You're a Britisher, aren't you, to judge by that accent of yours?"

He regarded me unblinkingly.

"It does so happen I was born in England. So what? I care

no more for England than it ever cared for me. Damn England. I'm stateless—as simple as that. Follow me?''

I let that go unanswered. Bella entered, wheeling a trolley which she set in front of me. The trolley held an assortment of alcoholic drinks which I ignored and some fresh lime juice which I drank avidly. The food was Korean, served straight from deep-freeze lunch trays and very palatable, especially to a man who had had nothing solid in his stomach for days.

"Do you know something about construction works, Mr. Roberts?" Hans asked.

"That's not important," the Master told him. "Go away and let me speak to Roberts alone. Get back to the harbor. Why are you hanging about here, anyway?"

"First you want me to paint signs, then you want me to work at the harbor—"

"Hans, this is no fun-fair. There's work to be done. Get down to that harbor when I tell you. You know the scum don't work well without you."

"You think I care?" Maastricht said, but he backed out all the same, casting black looks on the man in the chair.

When we were alone, the Master said dismissively, "I try to run a tight little ship. Now then, Mr. Calvert Roberts, we can have a talk, since you are here, however unwelcomely."

"Food's good. . . . After a week and more in an open boat, I tell you, a man is more than glad when Providence delivers him to terra firma, and to water, food, and human company—however unfriendly."

"Nobody has ever thanked Providence for being on this rock before."

"Maybe they should have tried it. . . . I want to discuss what you call this rock with you—"

He shook his head. "I want to discuss you. Never mind what you want. First things first. I have my priorities."

"Look, friend, you come on pretty heavy. You haven't even introduced yourself. You don't own me, remember. I'm not addressing you as 'Master'—what's your name?"

" 'Master' is my name here."

"You'll gain nothing by persisting in that attitude, I promise you. Your presence here, in the middle of a War Zone, is probably against military law, and carries severe penalties."
I continued to eat, while the orchestra continued to play and he wheeled himself fast about the room.

He returned to swerve in front of me, confronting me, and said, "If you find it so damned important, my name was

Dart. Mortimer Dart—though I'm now as nameless as I am stateless. As I am formless. There is no place for you on this island unless you submit to my authority."

"Why not cool it, Mr. Dart? I'm not challenging your authority, and I certainly don't require one slice of your little island. My intention is simply to get back to the States as soon as possible. My presence is required. ASASC—that's the Allied Space and Aerospace Corps, if you're out of touch —will be searching this whole area for survivors of the shuttle crash. I must use your radio to get in touch with ASASC HQ in San Diego, to have a message relayed to the President, letting him know I'm functional and pinpointing my present position. You will be compensated for any inconvenience."

He looked at me over one malformed shoulder, his lips compressed.

"According to you, you're an Undersecretary of State. A buddy of the President's, eh? Quite a big wheel. Important. It's not a tale I find likely—you, washed up here half dead. Prove you're who you claim."

"All my papers were lost in the *Leda* crash. Get on to ASASC, ask them if Undersecretary Roberts is missing. Or I can raise my own department on confidential wavelength —they'll be glad to identify me. You can also check on the names of the other guys in the crash. I can give them to you. I am real enough. The news I carry to the President is real enough."

He regarded me suspiciously. "What news?"

I looked at my watch and calculated. The war moved fast, even in its rather phony opening stages. Military movements which had been secret ten days ago on the Moon would be common knowledge on Earth by now.

"You follow the events of the war?"

He gestured toward the orchestra without removing his angry eyes from mine. "This I prefer. If men kill each other, so what?"

"Soviet ground, sea, and air forces are about to occupy Hokkaido and neighboring islands of Japan. They will thus command the Sea of Japan and sever sea links between the United States and China. I was returning from a conference on the Moon deciding the future conduct of war in the Japanese theater; it is essential I report back at once. Too much time has been lost to the enemy already."

Dart considered this sullenly. Then he spoke in a more

conciliatory tone. "I saw a bulletin this morning. A tremendous strike against Japanese cities and ports has just started. Give me some details about yourself, just to put me in the picture."

I clutched my knees. The nightmare, the closing agony of the twentieth century, was unrolling, and here I sat humoring some petty madman. . . . Briefly, I gave him a few details. Born on a farm in Connecticut, only son. Ambitious father of German descent, mother Scottish Presbyterian. Both sides of the family affluent. Father's connections enabled me to go into politics straight from university. A minor post in the Ammader Administration enabled me to go on a mission to Peking when the Russo–Chinese campaign along the Ussuri flared up. Was in Helsinki at the time of the Helsinki Incident marking the start of active Soviet expansionism. Escaped Finland and Europe with certain vital memory discs from NAPA HQ. Given governmental post shortly after, under President Willson.

To this account, Dart listened intently, head on one side. I felt that he was struggling to decide whether or not to believe my story. What I said was convincing, and near enough to the truth.

"You've been adventurous. Managed to move round the world, despite all the travel restrictions, East–West, North–South, all that red tape. . . . Your years have been active, according to you, up to the hilt. Real value for money, if you're not making it up." He sighed. "Just for the record, how old are you, Mr. Roberts?"

I took care not to let my growing impatience show.

"I'm thirty-five, getting a bit long in the tooth. Born 24th May, 1961. Married four times, divorced four times. No offspring. Anything else you want to know? I don't need a passport for Moreau Island, I guess?"

He made another circuit of the room, the machine taking a wide sweep, and bringing him back before me with an abrupt halt. Dart's face was grim, his brow wrinkled with a scowl.

"We are the same age, Mr. Roberts. Born on the same day of the same month. Is that a coincidence, a bad joke, or a frameup of some kind? While you've lived your life to the full—cities, women, that stuff—I've had to drag myself through existence on crutches, or in this cart, or worse. Same day. Glory for you, humiliation for me . . ."

"Glory . . ."

"You don't know the half of it, you four-limbed bastard."
The words were spoken almost without emphasis; it was just
something he habitually thought when confronted by ordinary people. He looked me in the eye as he said it. I dropped
my gaze. Dart's face, under its puffiness, was striking. He
had a heavy formidable skull with plenty of jaw and nose,
and a pair of deep-set malignant eyes with which to look out
at the world. His hair was dark and carelessly but rather
elegantly tumbled about his forehead. Maybe he was going
to run to fat.

"As you must have anticipated, I feel uncomfortable, Mr.
Dart. So our lives have been very different. Don't imagine
mine has not had its problems. Everyone's has. You don't
need me to explain how mysterious are the ways of God,
who communicates through suffering very often."

"God!" he echoed, and made a blasphemous remark. Although not only weak men swear, I consider the trait a sign
of weakness. "That's your mother's Presbyterian upbring-
ing, I suppose . . ."

It was time to change the subject. The orchestra had em-
barked on the last movement of Haydn's symphony, and
Bella almost surreptitiously wheeled the food trolley away.

I said to Dart, "I consider myself conversant with most
islands in the Pacific. Moreau Island I have not heard of.
How come? Who gave it its name?"

He countered with another question.

"Does the name Moreau ring any familiar bells with
you?"

I rubbed my chin.

"So happens, yes. I used to be a great admirer of the
scientific romances of H. G. Wells, who wrote *First Men in
the Moon* and *The Time Machine*. Wells also wrote a novel
about a Pacific island, nameless as I recall, on which a Dr.
Moreau practiced some unpleasant experiments on animals
of various kinds. Any connection?"

"You are on Dr. Moreau's island. This is that same island."

I laughed—a little uneasily, I have to admit.

"Come on, Dart. Moreau's is a purely fictitious island.
Wells was writing an allegory. I can distinguish between
reality and imagination, thanks."

"An ignorant boast, Mr. Roberts. Wells may have been
writing an allegory, but his island was firmly based on a real
one—just like the island on which Defoe's Robinson Crusoe

was shipwrecked was based on a real one. You know, Robinson Crusoe? Just like there was a real-life equivalent of Crusoe, so there was of Moreau. The real Moreau was a gentleman of some distinction at the Edinburgh Academy of Surgery, by name Mr. Angus McMoreau. He was a pupil of Thomas Huxley—Wells met him. His life is well documented. Wells did very little to camouflage the real situation, beyond some overdramatizing. In fact, McMoreau brought a lawsuit.''

''All of which must have been over a century ago.'' Dart evidently harbored some dangerous illusions. I disbelieved all he said, but thought it best to conceal my skepticism.

''Right, it was over a century ago, right,'' said Dart, laughing sourly. ''What difference does that make? McMoreau's experiments are still of relevance to research today. He was probing the borderland between human and animal nature, where the springs of modern man's behavior lie. Territorial imperatives, to name but one example I expect you're *au fait* with. Questions the scientific world tries to answer today by resort to piddling disciplines like paleontology and archeology, McMoreau tried to resolve through surgery. His methods were primitive but his ideas were valid. . . . He was a cute old nut case and no mistake.

''After Moreau's death, an assistant not mentioned in Wells' novel carried on his work for a number of years. Then he passed on as well, and the inhabitants of the island were left on their own to survive as best they could. It can't have been much of a picnic. As you know, they were hybrid stock, but some offspring were born, and they form the basis of the population as you see it today. They can trace their ancestry right back to McMoreau's times.''

The symphony finished. The orchestra bowed. Dart sat in his chair, staring out toward the lagoon as he finished speaking.

''In the Second World War, Japanese forces invaded most of the Pacific, including this island. No permanent detachment was based here. Then, after the Japanese surrender, knowledge of the island came into American hands. Its native name is Narorana, by the way. Which means private. A scientific detachment was sent to investigate and—''

He paused. Something in the courtyard outside had caught his eye. He bowled over to the window. I also went to look, so impressed was I by the look of absolute fury on his face.

Bella alone was to be seen. She stood against the palisade.

For a moment I thought she was talking to herself; then it became apparent that she must be speaking to someone on the other side of the fortification.

"How many times have I told her—"

Dart was moving again, charging through the door and along the corridor. "Da Silva! Da Silva!" he called. His chair had a turn of speed to match his anger. He appeared outside, closely followed by a slender, dark-complexioned man in a lab coat who I guessed was the hastily summoned Da Silva. I saw Dart reach for a whip clamped to the outside of his chair. Then I started running.

When I got outside, it was to see him striking the wretched Bella repeatedly across her shoulders. She cowered under the lash but made no attempt to run away until I shouted, whereupon she showed a good turn of speed and slipped inside by a farther door.

The man in the white coat grasped my arm without a great deal of conviction and I easily brushed him aside. I seized Dart's whip and flung it to the far end of the compound.

"You dare interfere—This is my island—" Dart's face turned a patchy yellow.

"They aren't your people to do what you like with—"

"They are my people—"

"You do not own their souls—"

"They have no souls, they're animals—"

"Animals deserve better than that. You and I are going to quarrel, Dart, unless you keep your temper in check. I can see you feel you have reason to hate the world, and I'm sorry, but I will not stand by and see you—"

"You fool, I'll throw you out of here if you speak to me like that! You dare attack me?"

He was far from subdued by my action. His face was a study in malice. Moreover, I had by no means disarmed him by wrenching his whip away. He seemed to be literally well armed. Whatever disaster had struck him, I saw now that he had had his arms as well as his legs replaced, though the loose-fitting garment he wore made this hard to discern. Three pairs of arms were clamped on both sides of his chair, making him look somewhat like a plastic-and-metal spider. Some of these six interchangeable appendages ended in very odd hands indeed; at least two of them looked like lethal weapons.

But he mastered his wrath and said, "Just be warned.

Come back inside; I wish to finish speaking to you. Da Silva, back to the labs.''

His chair bore him speedily back into the room we had left, and I followed.

Dart flipped off the vision on his huge screen. Only music flowed through the room—a quartet by Shostakovich.

"These people have to be kept under stern control—as you will understand when you have been here a little longer.'' He spoke without looking at me.

I was still angry and would not reply. When Dart spoke again, it was in a vein of explanation, although the tone of his voice gave no hint of apology.

"The truth is, Roberts, that I'm vexed to be interrupted in my work by you or anyone else. My work here has gone through three stages. The first stage was merely to duplicate Moreau's original experiments, the second—well, never mind that. Suffice it to say, cutting the cackle, that I'm now into the culminating third stage. All the early crudities of approach have been set aside, junked—finished. I'm beyond all that. I'm discovering . . . I'm discovering *the relativity of flesh* . . .

"The phrase means nothing to you, Roberts. But believe me, all these years of pain—and pained thought—suffering is nothing unless you learn from it—I am the Einstein of a revolutionary biology . . .''

He flashed a look at me.

"I'm listening," I said.

He laughed. I saw again that dark and troubled thing in him. "I know you're listening, man. Mr. Roberts, I want you on my side and don't know how to get you there. I'm not another Moreau. You've decided already you hate me, haven't you?''

"I couldn't take the way you treated Bella.''

"Listen, I'm not another Moreau. He was a monster in many ways, a tyrant. I'm a victim. Try and dig that concept. A victim. Look!''

With a quick movement of his chin, he struck at a button on his right shoulder. So far as I had noticed it, I regarded it as a button securing his loose-flowing tunic. It was more than that. There was a sharp snap, a whirr of servomechanisms, and Dart's right arm slid off and clamped itself against the side of the chair.

Another brusque chin movement, and he pushed the tunic from his shoulder so that it fell away.

I saw his real arm.

It was not an arm. It was scarcely a hand. Four flexible digits like fingers sprouted from the shoulder joint. He swerved the chair so that I could see the detail, and the puckering of flesh where a shape almost like a hand had formed under the smooth nub of shoulder.

"On the other side, it's a bit more grotesque. And my phalanges and metatarsal bones grow out of deformed femurs—that's what I've got for legs. And I have a penile deformity."

His voice as he spoke was throaty and the eyes of this Einstein of a revolutionary biology were bright with moisture.

Although I regarded him stolidly, my face unmoving, I had to fight an unexpected urge to apologize. Why the healthy body should apologize to the defective, I do not know. That's not part of my philosophy.

"Why are you so anxious to gain my pity?"

He leaned sideways. The little fingers pressed a button inside the artificial arm. It moved back into place again, snapping when it was correctly positioned. The tiny sound provoked him to nod to himself almost complacently.

He was in control of himself, as his voice showed when he spoke again. "Back in all those crummy years when I was a kid, I used to go on reading jags, Mr. Roberts. All sorts of crap I read. Not old H. G. Wells, I don't mean. Dostoevsky, Nietzsche, and a lot more, as well as technical books. A French writer called Gide compares Dostoevsky and Nietzsche. He finds them very alike, and do you know what he puts on about them? He says that Nietzsche was jealous of Jesus Christ, envied him to the point of madness, whereas Dostoevsky was struck with humility and regarded Jesus as a superman. You know what? As those two writers regarded Jesus Christ, so I regarded ordinary human beings —holding both attitudes at the same time. Because I was born monstrous and deformed, Mr. Roberts. I was a thalidomide kid. Remember thalidomide?"

I remembered the thalidomide scandal well. The drug had been manufactured as a tranquilizer by a German company and licensed by chemical firms all over the world. The side effects of the drug had not been properly researched; its teratogenicity had only become apparent when babies were born deformed. When the drug was administered to women in the early stages of pregnancy, it had the power of passing through the placental barrier and malforming the growth of the fetus. From eight to ten thousand children were born defective in various parts of the globe.

What made me recall the case so clearly was that, over twenty years ago, when there was a court case in Canada regarding the amount of compensation to be paid one of the thalidomide children, my mother had said to me, "Cal, you were born at the time when thalidomide was available all round the world. We are just lucky that the States has sane laws about testing drugs—so that when I went to Doc Harris for a tranquilizer during pregnancy, he prescribed something safe. Otherwise you might have been born without your proper limbs, like other babies your age in England and elsewhere."

I said to Dart, "That whole case was a piece of criminal negligence." I could but stare at him, ashamed to move my eyes away.

"My mother was prescribed Distaval, as thalidomide was called in England, and used it for a week only. One week! That week covered the forty-first to the forty-eighth day of her pregnancy.When I was born, I had these severe abnormalities on which you now gaze with such pleasure.

"If the doctors had had any sense, they would never have let me live."

"But you've survived . . ."

"I'll leave you to think about what survival means in the circumstances. Life's not been much of a fun-fair, Mr. Roberts."

He was gone, skidding away on two wheels. I stood where I was in the center of the room. I put my hands in my pockets. My brain was refusing to think.

Shostakovich was bringing his affairs to an enigmatic close.

It was not until the next morning that Mortimer Dart appeared again.

By that time, my strength had returned to me and I had gone through a good deal of anxious heart-searching. I had also met Heather Landis.

Dart's last remark had moved me; he had invited me to look into his life, that life of the same duration as mine (or so he claimed) but made so very different by physical accident. I had one way of understanding the sort of existence —I mean the sort of mental existence—he had led, by considering the uses to which he had put the island. Those uses (though I had only a sketchy notion of them so far) constituted a fairly broad indication of the sort of man with whom I was dealing.

I found myself virtually a prisoner. Although the house contained several doors, they were mostly locked. The only rooms to which I had access were my room with its attendant bathroom and the main room I have described. I could get into the compound, but that was of little avail since it did not lead to the rest of the house and the outer doors leading to the village were kept locked.

Beyond my captivity, the ocean and the daylight fulfilled their predestined functions without touching me. I felt myself as firmly imprisoned by the Master as if I were held captive in his mind.

Confinement was no new thing to me. Although I considered myself a well-traveled man, I was one of the late twentieth-century version of that species; I had been all round the world and to the Moon in my official capacity, yet most of that travel had been done behind metal plating, and most of the destinations had been security-shrouded rooms. Although I had plenty of muscle, my real strength lay in my nerve. I was a good negotiator when called upon—and negotiation calls upon use of the backside.

When dark came down over Moreau Island, extraordinary cries and whoops sounded from the direction of the village. I went into the compound to see what I could see, but the walls were too high for me to observe much more than the chilly blue-white eyes of lights burning above the deserted quayside. As I turned to go inside again, a figure crossed the shadowy room I had just left.

"Hey!" I called, and ran in after it. It had been a girl— not Bella.

There was only a desk lamp burning by an instrument panel.

By its light, dimly across the other side of the room, I saw a small deformed girl.

"Who are you?" I asked.

"Hi there," she said. She turned and switched more lights on.

"Who are you?" I asked in a different tone. The girl was small, certainly, but perfectly formed. Her hair was long, dark, and curly, and hung about her shoulders; tricks that the shadows played on it had led me to believe for a moment that she was a hunchback. Now I saw that was not so. She was of slender build, and wore a plain loose saffron-colored tunic and a pair of dark nylon trousers, with sandals on her bare feet. Her most remarkable feature was a pair of enormous dark eyes which regarded me with the surprised gaze of some nocturnal animal, a tarsier or a loris.

"I'm Heather," she said. "I work for the Master."

I moved closer to her. She backed away.

"I'd prefer if you'd keep a little distance between the two of us, Mr. Calvert Roberts." Although wary, her tone was also slightly flirtatious.

"You American? You're not one of the natives?"

"You have a great way of handing out a compliment!"

"It was your accent—look, I don't want to offend Dart—after all, his boys pulled me out of the drink—but the sooner I can get a radio message to San Diego, the better. Can you help?"

She put an index finger to her mouth and nibbled at the nail. "I hear you're lucky to be alive. Sorry, passing messages just isn't my thing."

"Then I want to speak to Dart—or Maastricht, or Da Silva."

"Da Silva lives in the lab. Hans is drunk as usual. You know, if that guy would only make the effort, he could throw off his alcoholic addiction just like that. Fundamentally, he is very nice."

"Let me speak to someone else then. I can't waste any more time."

She put her arms akimbo and summed me up with her big eyes. There was too much conscious charm in the gesture for my taste. "So you were the only one who survived ten days in an open boat. Why do you imagine you alone survived and your friends did not?"

"They happened to be blown up, else they'd have survived. They were real tough. Look, lady, it's nice to see you—will you show me to the radio?"

"Do you think I would have survived in your boat?"

I was growing impatient with the conversation. She—Heather—was prowling about the room now, laying a hand on chairbacks and desks as she passed them. She was very graceful, and I observed the little plump buttocks in her trousers.

I said, "I'd guess you'd be better in bed than in an open boat."

Thinking back afterward I could see that it was not the kind of remark to make to that kind of lady. The tight trousers misled me. She took my intended compliment as an insult of a particular male kind and, being of a tricky temperament, made me pay for it during the rest of my time on the island.

She glared at me. "What makes you think I couldn't survive in an open boat? I've survived plenty, believe me. You have to be tough to exist here."

She sounded belligerent but was preparing to escape.

"No offense intended. Don't fly off the handle. What exactly is your function?"

At that, she prowled nearer to me, still looking unfriendly.

"They fished you out of the ocean, feller—what right do you have to question me? Let's just say that I play Man Friday to the Master's Robinson Crusoe, is that okay?"

Forcing a smile, I said, "It doesn't tell me what you're doing here."

"What I'm doing is bringing your supper, since Bella's nowhere to be found. . . . It's in your bedroom." Unease showed beneath her display of fighting spirit, and I thought it was the first time she had answered one of my questions directly. "I never met an Undersecretary of State before, so I wanted to see what you were like. You're no different from anyone else."

As she made for the door into the corridor, I grasped one of her slim wrists. She must have been expecting it. She twisted in such a way that pain sprang up my arm and I let go of her. I caught one mocking glance from her large eyes; then she was gone.

Over my cold Korean meal, I wondered how much I was being manipulated. Someone like Dart would have a powerful compulsion to gain as full a control over his environment as possible; to that end, he could have no better setting than a small island. It remained to be seen how much the fey Heather was her own agent or something Dart controlled. What was her remark about having perfect control over herself?

Although I regarded what I had seen of the events on the island with misgiving, my interest lay elsewhere, and my duty was to report back, and then get back, to the center of things as soon as possible. There was a war on, and I was part of it. I went to bed in a moderately bad temper and spent an immoderately bad night.

4

A Quick Swim in the Lagoon

When breakfast came, it was Bella who brought it, not Heather. She sidled into my room with a tray and would, I believe, have slunk out without speaking had I not called to her. Her heavy head came over her shoulder and she regarded me with those smoldering feline eyes.

"Bella, will you tell your Master that I wish to speak to him? I wish him to send a message by radio and then I intend to quit his establishment. I will stay in the village until my relief party comes. Tell him that."

"You no like this place?"

"Do you, Bella?"

She considered the question, looking down at the floor. At last, she said, "You Four Legs Long but you no like see me get whip last yest'day."

"Tell Master what I say, Bella—he won't whip you."

"You no got whip."

She went. *You no got whip!* was that her way of commending me, or did she speak contemptuously? Was she telling me to mind my own business? I had no idea.

When the Master came, rolling quickly up in his self-propelled chair, I was awaiting him. I held out a sheet of paper.

"Here's a signal to ASASC HQ, informing them that I am

alive and stating my whereabouts. I'll ask you to add grid references for this island. May I remind you that there is a war on, and that it is your duty as a British citizen to assist the Co-Allied cause by beaming this message immediately. Meanwhile, I'll take up your offer of yesterday and leave these premises. I can stay somewhere down in the village until the relief party comes.''

"Stay somewhere in the village? That's good. You won't find any Holiday Inn to put up at. No way.''

"I'm not here on vacation.''

Dart looked at me curiously. Then he snatched up the paper with prosthetic fingers and swung round in his chair. ''If it's local color you're after, you'll get a basinful of that right enough. You obviously don't care for my company—perhaps the company in the *kampong* will suit your tastes. Though they don't play Haydn down there, you'll find.''

I didn't answer that. I followed him outside.

When we reached the outer gate, he raised the seat of his chair electrically until he was high enough to insert a magnetic key in a lock set well up the gate. Then he spun a wheel, as I had seen him doing on the outside of the compound. The gate rolled open. I was free to go.

"See you,'' I said, tipping a finger at him.

He sat watching me, still and alert as a toad, as I walked through the gate and out into the sunshine.

The view under the trees was striking. The eye was led under an avenue of foliage toward the glittering waters of the lagoon, with the village nestling modestly among palm trees on the far side. The sound of the ocean pounding against rocks came clear to me; it was the permanent sound of Moreau Island, and would remain so, long after men had gone. I could not help contrasting my surroundings with the silent and austere landscape of Luna.

But I was preoccupied with thoughts of Mortimer Dart, the Master, and the kind of man he was. I had yet to grasp the situation on the island, and that I determined to do. The whole concept of an island ruled over by one man was an anachronism—something that the big powers would not tolerate. There were certain matters here I could investigate before the rescue party came to pick me up.

I was not entirely sure that Dart intended to transmit my message. To make certain, I would send a cable from the village. Or so I told myself, making a grave error of judgment.

I started optimistically toward the village. I had gone half a dozen paces when a figure leaped from the bushes. It ran across my path and stopped beside me, panting and laughing.

It was Bernie the Dog Man, showing his teeth in nothing but an amiable way and pushing his face with its large moist eyes toward mine. He tapped his chest as when we first met and said, "Your name Bernie—good boy, good man. Speak only with speech. Never eat filth, no, no!"

"Hello, Bernie. You still remember me, do you?"

His whole body wriggled with pleasure and he moved as close to me as he could. "Ha, many nighttimes! You Four Limbs Long, well made. Good boy, good man, take out of the big waters all wet. Like fish, yes, good. Use the hands, speak only with speech. Don't be bad or need Whip any more."

As I began to move on, he kept pace with me, still talking, giving me watchful sideways glances which reminded me of the hulking George, although there was none of George's menace in Bernie's evasive stare.

"Are you coming with me to the village, Bernie?"

"Are you coming with you, Bernie, yes! Good speech, many nighttimes! Good, Bernie good, good boy—got little hands and arms like Master. I come with you in my body, good. Not need Whip any more, you'll see. One, two, three, five. . . . Green, yellow, plate. You Bernie, you not Master, you friend, you good boy . . ."

With such conversation to enlighten us, we came down to the harbor.

When I had passed this way on my arrival on Moreau Island, my exhaustion had been too great for me to take in much of my surroundings. I stood and regarded them now with disappointment. The harbor and the village were poor things; proximity to what I had regarded as a picturesque South Sea island retreat brought nothing but disillusion.

The harbor was constructed of concrete-filled sandbags, the fabric of which had long ago rotted away. A wooden walk stretched a few yards out over the water, but I would not have wanted to trust myself to it. Two battered old landing craft—one of which had been used in my rescue, I did not doubt—were moored there. The place reeked of neglect.

As for the village! In the noonday light, only a row of half a dozen palms, sloping out over the water, lent it a touch of beauty. It was no more than a collection of hovels. Some of the hovels were constructed from natural materials such as palm leaves. Others were built with the castoffs of Western civilization—ancient jerry cans, corrugated iron, old packing cases, rusting automobiles. All were miserable in the extreme. One or two brutish faces peered out of doorways, not moving in the heat. My expectations about sending cables died at once.

The only sign of activity, or of intelligence, was round on the other side of the lagoon, on the right of where I stood with Bernie. There groups of natives were bending their backs, a concrete mixer was chugging, a mobile crane swung blocks of stone out into the green water.

Sunshine enveloped me. Sweat trickled down my backbone. I stood gazing at the scene, taking in all the parsimonious evidences of mankind set against a natural prodigality. I stared down at the concrete of the quayside beneath my feet. The concrete was laid in prefabricated slabs, many of which had been broken at the corners during the process of laying. Cracks ran like lines on an automobile map, creating cartographic sketches of obliterated cities; weeds, forcing their way among the fissures and avenues, represented vegetation surviving in microcosmic Hiroshimas. All directions ultimately led nowhere. The primitive roadway, to my anxious mind, formed a diagram of what was in process; I saw I also had a miniature battle on my hands here. I would have to overcome Dart if I was ever to leave Moreau Island.

I began walking slowly along the edge of the lagoon, oppressed with a thunderous sense of fate which I tried to tell myself was nothing more than the receding tide of my weakness. The chug-chug of the concrete mixer ahead, the swinging arm of the crane, seemed to offer something stable in my uncertain state. As I advanced, I heard my name called. A hand waved from the crane. My pace became more positive in response. The arm of the crane halted in midswing, and Maastricht jumped down.

He strolled toward me, bare-chested, riot gun slung over his right shoulder.

"You're jack-of-all-trades, I see, Mr. Maastricht."

"Nobody else to do it if I don't. Can't leave it to this gang of brutes to do sensible work." He evaded my gaze as he spoke by glancing at the natives he referred to.

"There must be other—well, white men on the island."

"Warren—no, no, there's no person else, just the Master

and me. And Da Silva." He ran a hand across his face, as if
to wipe out a mistake he had nearly made. "I thought you
understood the setup. You're slow to catch on, you a Yan-
kee politician."

"My brain's been boiling in my skull for too many days,
Mr. Maastricht."

"Call me Hans, for heaven's sake, man. You stuffy politicians, I don't know. Come and have a drink."

"I don't drink. I thought I told you. You're slow to catch
on."

He looked almost straight at me and then grinned. He
pulled a crumpled pack of mescahales from his pocket and
lit one. "Bet you don't smoke either?"

"Correct. It's a vile habit."

"You're not drinking, not smoking—what *do* you do, Mr.
Roberts?"

I outstared him, and he dropped his eyes, muttering.

"I'm not such a bastard as I might appear." Then he
turned and kicked out with one foot, catching the wretched
Bernie on one flank. "You, Bernie, what the hell are you
doing? Four Limbs Long, Song Gone Wrong, remember.
Back to work."

Bernie departed, yelling and hopping. Behind us, the work
crew labored slowly and clumsily on. I saw George sitting
on a slab of stone, eyeing them darkly from under his hat,
and gathered that he was the foreman of the gang.

"Yes, as I was saying, I'm not such a bastard. It's just
that the Master—Dart—I get the custom of calling him Master—he brings out the worst. I used to be a painter, in my
good days, bygone."

"An artist, eh? Amsterdam's a good city for artists."

"No, no, you misunderstand, no Rembrandt. I paint
houses, inside or out. I have three men work under me. Now
only animals! Come and see what we are doing now here."

He showed me how they were straightening out the curve
of the lagoon at that point by throwing in stone, so as to
make a proper mooring for small ships.

"That little quay you passed was built by the Japanese,
way back in the last world war, when I was a little baby.
Here the water is much deeper, to make a better berth. You
see the fish?"

We stood looking over the edge. The water was a clear
green. A million little fish glittered in it, all the way down to
sand.

"Where do you get the blocks of stone? It doesn't look as if you've been blasting the cliff."

"No, we don't blast the cliff." He leaned in the shadow of the crane, picking up his familiar bottle and taking a swig. "See, we have an underground reservoir for fresh water. You get to it from inside the palisade. Much stones. That was all dug out by hand, by the Beast People."

"The Beast People!"

"You see, the secret is to keep them working, Calvert—Mr. Roberts. You must keep them working. Now I'm a Marxist, myself, unlike the Master, who's a fascist pig, so I know all about the proles. What was I going to be saying? Yes, that's right. You keep them working. First they dig out the reservoir, take several years, now they build the new quay with the stones."

"I'd like to ask you a lot of questions about Dart, Hans. But first of all, can I send a radio message from anywhere here?"

"Through the Master's transmitters. No other way, of course."

"That's a little awkward, because I have just moved out."

His expression became very gloomy and worried.

"That's bad. However, he is very consistent—no, I mean he is not consistent. I will speak to him for you. You must be inside by nightfall, of course."

"How so?"

He looked askance at me. He took another swig from the bottle. He looked at the selection of burly and hairy backs near us, at the little eyes that forever furtively regarded us over hunched shoulders. Then he shrugged expressively.

"They're dangerous?" I asked in a low voice.

He laughed roughly to show how stupid he thought my question—too stupid to answer. Instead, he took another drink. "You'll end up a drinking man before you're here a week, chum. I bet you!" I could see he was relapsing into the sullen mood in which I had found him on our first meeting.

"I don't intend to be here a week," I said.

He gave me an odd look, and then heaved himself back into the crane.

I walked on, past the work group, to the extreme tip of the land, where the lagoon met the ocean. The water of the lagoon was green; the water of the ocean was blue. I saw how sheer the cliffs were, and knew that they went on down into deep waters. There was no continental shelf here. Anything that fell into the Pacific would keep on falling for a long way.

The air smelled good. I breathed deep, feeling strength return.

I was in a position where I could see the north coast of Moreau Island, curving to either side, since the lagoon lay roughly in the middle of its length. The island was boomerang-shaped. The high cliffs lay to the east of the lagoon; on the west, they were replaced by a broken shoreline. Out to sea was nothing, except for one sizable rock, crowned by a stunted palm, standing about a kilometer off the eastern tip of the island. Nothing else but unbroken horizon, not even a cloud. The Moon never looked quite so empty. And the empty lives about me . . .? From that thought, I turned away.

While I sat staring out toward the horizon, beyond which a world war was gathering strength, the dog-like Bernie crept up to me again. He panted and groveled at my feet without daring to speak. So isolated was I that I felt glad to have him there.

"Good boy, good man," I said.

A siren shrilled. For a while, I wondered if an air attack were imminent—the work gang dropped whatever they were doing and took to their heels, shouting and bellowing as they went. Bernie jumped up and started whining, although he did not leave my side.

The stampede headed round the rim of the lagoon, making for the village. One of the natives fell, to scamper on unhurt. Maastricht jumped down from his crane and called to me.

"That's lunchtime. Now is where I switch on the music!"

He went across to a metal locker like a small sentry box which stood near the water, opened it, and pressed a switch. Drumming filled the air.

Amplifiers were dotted here and there over the island. Some were fixed to the lamp standards round the lagoon, with a concentration of them in the village.

A series of jingles burst from the amplifiers, filling the air.

> One thing unites us all—that's Love!
> Come on, there, Baby, don't matter the Shape—
> Be Beastly now, rock, push, and shove,
> Wolf, leopard, jackal, with man, bull, and ape!

Maastricht came up to me, laughing at the expression of disgust on my face.

"So we train 'em and keep 'em happy at the same time. Break down that narrow gap between human and animal." He launched a kick at Bernie, who was slinking close to me. "Get out, you brute! There's no food here!"

"Leave him alone! Why should you treat him like that? Bernie, here, come on, good man, stay with me if you want!"

Whimpering, Bernie came back toward me and crept fearfully behind my back, where he remained to make quiet growling curses at the Netherlander.

Maastricht's face had gone brick-red. He clutched the butt of his riot gun without unslinging it. "Let me warn you, hero! You are just new here! Keep at my good side. That's what I say—keep at my good side! You are already enough in peril. You do not know the Beast People like I. Why you think Dart turns you out? Because he hopes they tear you apart, so he then don't got any problem with you, right?"

"You degrade these people by brutality, but they don't look dangerous."

His anger left him abruptly, and he turned away to avoid my eyes. "Only after nightfall do things get dangerous on Moreau Island, hero. If he want you back and locked in by then, it is not for your sake, don't worry! It is so that these friends of yours don't go amok with taste of blood, savvy! Ask Bernie!"

He climbed back into his crane and began to eat his lunch.

The singing continued raucously, echoing across island and ocean.

> Go ape now, Baby, have yourself a ball—
> Get with the loving, forget the Shape,
> Groove it on in a laughing fall,
> Wolf, leopard, jackal, with man, bull, and ape!

I went over to the crane and asked Maastricht, "Why give them this muck? Why not Haydn?"

He spluttered with laughter over his bottle. He was tapping one boot to the rhythm.

"Jesus, but you are an idealist! I forgive you, hero—I was an idealist once. I even went to Church. Haydn? Papa Haydn? Why vex them with things they don't understand?

You got to dress up smart for Haydn, right, hero! This is a utopia, not a prison camp." He bellowed with laughter and then repeated what was possibly a favorite line. "This is a utopia, not a prison camp."

There was no sense in arguing with him. I folded my arms and leaned against the machine, looking up at the sky where fulmars sailed.

Maastricht passed me down a coconut still encased in its green husk and said, more reasonably, "You understand the Master is content as long as nobody make trouble. His interest is in the similarity of human and animal. Form and attitude determine behavior—he will tell you if you ask him."

"Moreau practiced vivisection in Wells' novel." As I spoke, I was watching three seals, or at any rate seal-like creatures, come swimming into the lagoon from the open sea. "He tortured human shapes out of leopards and other animals—a peculiarly nineteenth-century occupation, it seemed, until the process was virtually reversed in the concentration camps of the last world war. Dart says he duplicated Moreau's experiments. Research is too kind a name for it. He is using a scalpel simply as an instrument of torture."

"You God-freaks are all the same! You condemn without bothering to find out facts. Pfhah! The Master's not Moreau. Give him his damned due. Time has moved on since that crude stuff."

"Nobody who behaves—"

"I show you something, hero! Watch this!" He pointed toward the three seal creatures and then leaned out of the cab, calling to them. Bernie, excited, dashed to the edge of the water, inserted fingers in both cheeks and whistled. The seals turned in our direction.

Maastricht flung a piece of food into the water to hasten their progress, but they moved slowly. As they neared, I saw that their faces were surprisingly human, though obscured by long flowing black hair. Finally, they rested against the rocks, shaking water out of their eyes, and calling, "Hello, Hans!"—while at the same time looking warily at me.

Bernie was hopping up and down, trying to communicate with them. "Speak only with speech, come out from water, yes. New Four Limbs Long, good, good man. No Bearded One, two, three, five . . ."

They gave him good-natured glances, but were dismissive,

too, as if they accepted that Maastricht's companions were not to their taste. Their faces were rounded and not unlike seals; their noses were flattened, their skins very dark, and their eyes had an epicanthic fold which made them resemble Japanese. Their bodies were shaped like human bodies, except that they had four flipper-like appendages instead of arms and legs.

"Get a close look, hero! What do you think they are?" Hans shouted.

"I am looking . . ." I could see that the appendages differed on the three creatures; one of them had a vestigial leg. They playfully splashed water at Bernie, then dived and began clumsily to swim across to the village, evidently more hopeful of finding food there.

Maastricht took a large swig on his bottle, choked, and said, not precisely looking at me, "Those are humans, hero. They are humans, and no scalpel has been near them. And that's what happened to the Master, just the same thing. That's what the Master really looks like."

He drank again, letting liquid run down his chin into his beard. He shook his head.

I sat down in the dusty shade of the crane. Bernie came and sat comfortingly close to me on one side. Maastricht jumped clumsily down from the footplate and squatted on my other side.

"The Master's got reason for cutting up nasty now and again, hasn't he? That's what your bloody God did to him, see?"

There were many replies to that. Instead, I pointed to the three creatures still wallowing their way across the lagoon and said, "And what did your bloody Master do to them?"

"Whatever he did, hero, he had a license from Above, didn't he?" He laughed stupidly and pointed up where fulmars wheeled above us. He seemed to pull himself back from the edge of drunkenness and said, with cold sense, "You make me drink more than usual, hero, you savvy that? I guess it means I feel guilty. I'm not such a bastard. . . . Look, let me tell you. See, the Master's interested in the plasticity of flesh—human and animal, and shapes unthought of . . ." His voice tailed off. After a while, he said, "There's two hours' siesta. Let's take a swim, then a sit in the shade, and talk. Okay?"

We stripped naked and dived into the lagoon. The water felt as beautiful as it looked. I had gone in to humor him, and now rejoiced in the element I had so recently hated. Maastricht never ventured far from the rocks, on which he had left his riot gun close to the water's edge for easy access, but I was impelled to swim out to the middle and thence to the mouth of the lagoon. There I floated, treading water, staring across the ocean which had so recently attempted to swallow me up. A sort of anguish rose in me; I thought that ever afterward I would have a fear of wide expanses of water, as I had never had a fear of limitless space.

While I floated there, the three Seal Men came splashing up to me. They seemed playful, but were unsmiling and wary, and I disliked being surrounded by them so much at first that I caught myself looking round for Hans and his gun.

I saw that one of the three Seal People was a woman. She was the most sportive, leaping up so that I could see her delicate breasts, diving to reveal the cleft and scut of hair between her flipper-feet.

"Where do you live?" I asked her.

"Oh, live, yes—you Four Limbs Long, good, good man." She said something laughingly to her companions, who swam about rather soberly. She had strong white teeth. She counted up to ten. "Many times, what you like. Green, yellow—speak always with speech. You live with Master."

"Yes, I live with Master. Where do you live? Where do you three live?"

"One, two, three, live, yes, where I live. It's not a fun-fair. They two men, me girl. Pretty girl."

I was amused that she had picked up Dart's English expression about life not being a fun-fair.

The two men began to beat about in the water. Although the amplifiers were still booming a jingle across the water to us, one of the Seal Men began to sing, clearly and in a good accent:

I've a wife and a lover in fair London Town
And tonight she a widow will be, will be, will be. . . .

The girl brushed against me and caught me by my hair with the fingers that sprouted from her shoulder. Her face pressed into mine. I put an arm about her, feeling her naked and rubbery little body against me. She pushed, and the others were there pushing. I went under the water, kicking out to escape, but the Seal Girl came with me. Her eyes were open, and her mouth. She was excited. We came plunging up, blowing water, she giggling heartily. She dived again, and I knew I was being examined underwater.

One of the men jerked a shoulder and pointed with a look toward the palm-crowned rock I had observed earlier, standing a kilometer away from the end of Moreau Island.

"Home," he said. "Is good fun, home. Catch fish, dive. We go, no trouble, one, two, three, four. Yes, hero?"

"You live on that rock?"

"Live, yes, live rock. No trouble. One, two, three, girl. 'Get with the loving, forget the Shape . . .' "

We were moving forward in the warm water together. It was like talking to dolphins. The girl was laughing in my face; her bright dark eyes, her white teeth, the touch of her body, had an intense impact on me. Suddenly, I felt a colder area in the water. Looking down, I saw that we were moving away from the lip of the lagoon, entering the ocean proper. The water hue changed abruptly from green to a deep blue. We were coming over steep gradients, where the neck of the island tumbled down sheer into the unplumbed abyss.

"No, no farther!" I was afraid. The understanding came that I had been ill and was still not fully in command of myself.

I broke away from the girl and swam back toward the crane, trying not to hear their jeering calls and whistles. The episode had shaken me; in more than one sense, I had been on the brink of something unfathomable.

The island closed round me. I swam to the shore, trod water, pulled myself up by where my clothes lay. Bernie was guarding them; he held out his hand, but I pushed him off and lay down to let the sun dry me, shaking.

A few paces away, also prone, Maastricht said, "Jesus, I thought you were off then, hero! That might be the one route for escape."

"It's difficult to tell how intelligent these people are. Their mastery of the language doesn't amount to much." I tried to stop my voice trembling.

"Those Seal People are smart cookies, you understand. They are the only ones who have escaped the Master, apart from—no, the only ones. He has all of their defects. He don't got arms and legs. One shoulder blade is missed. That's the thalidomide drug. I knew a Chinese man in Jakarta who had lost both his legs as a child, and he—"

Maastricht launched himself into a complicated anecdote. I had no desire to listen. The understanding that had burst upon me—that I had suffered more than I knew from my long exposure in the ocean, followed by the unnatural shocks of this island—took possession of me with all the force of novelty. I needed to think about it. Still trembling in every limb, I got dressed as quickly as I could.

In his maundering way, Maastricht had reverted to the topic of Dart.

"See, hero, he had a struggle to manhood, too. But he was lucky. He won by legal suit—no, by lawsuit, he won many compensations from the pharmaceutical company who make the drug. So he could come here and start work. He does not do that old scalpel business like you think. Only drugs, to change the fetus in the womb, savvy? There were all kinds of animals here, left over from Moreau's time. Also some Japanese fisherman families. Your three swimming friends, they're triplets born to a Jap girl who took the drug in her second and third month pregnant."

I got up and walked away. I did not want to talk.

"It gives something to think about, don't it, hero?" Maastricht called.

I made no answer.

"Don't think about it, Cal," he called. Without looking back, I could imagine him upending the bottle in his fleshy mouth.

5

A Chance
to Think
Things Over

In my troubled state of mind, I had to keep walking—walking away from Maastricht and his unhappy preoccupations. I needed somewhere where I could think straight, in peace. I headed eastward, which soon entailed going uphill. Bernie scampered by my side, making consoling noises. Birds hopped before us into the pale undergrowth.

When I came to consider it, I realized that I knew few details about the administration of the Pacific; the subject lay outside my department; but I felt convinced that the setting up of the United Oceans Consortium in the eighties to conserve and control the world hydrosphere precluded anyone from establishing his own private hell as Dart had done. Was the island never visited by UOC patrols? Had the U.S. Navy never investigated?

On a deeper level, I contemplated the political realities that hid behind fancy labels like the United Oceans Consortium. For the UOC had been established by the United States, China, and Japan, together with several satellite states such as Singapore, to contain spreading Soviet domination of Pacific waters. The Soviets, with their reluctant but vital allies in the Middle East, now controlled the Mediterranean (traditional base of sea power), the North Sea, and

the Atlantic. The war was being fought to a great extent over
the last free ocean. That both Chinese and Japanese compa-
nies were extracting vital oil from coastal oil fields only ac-
centuated the bitterness of the struggle.

Moreau Island, without U.S. or UOC protection, could
provide an ideal supply base for the giant Soviet nuke subs,
situated as it was within strike distance of Australia and not
all that far from the important base of Singapore.

As soon as I returned to Washington, I would see that the
matter of Moreau Island was thoroughly investigated. And
that, I perceived, was precisely what Dart expected me to
do. Would he then send my radio message? Or would he
attempt to detain me here, either keeping me as a kind of
prisoner, or seeing that something far more permanent happened to me, as Maastricht had suggested?

The answer to such questions depended on the extent of
Dart's ruthlessness, and on the extent to which his experiments went beyond the bounds of normal human conduct.
My state of health had been more enfeebled than I had realized until now; it had led me to pretend that very little was
the matter—that for instance the wretched "village" was an
ordinary village in which facilities for cabling, rooms to let,
and so on were available. No one had attempted to mislead
me in these matters; I had unknowingly misled myself.

The account I have so far given of myself shows me, I
realize, in a poor light. Normally, I can rely on myself to
behave with perception, command, and decision. Since I
had been dragged half dead into Maastricht's boat, my actions had been feeble in every way. In particular, I had managed to ignore the dreadful realities round me.

I sat on a boulder in the speckled shade and Bernie settled
beside me, gazing up at my face. After a moment, he put a
hand on my knee and uttered some of his propitiatory nonsense. I stared down at his stunted limb in pity and horror,
forcing myself, now that I was back to my senses, to experience the full realization of what Bernie was. He was a
welding of animal and human, the grotesque result of laboratory experiment. Similar specimens inhabited the island,
and I walked among them. An intense shaking took my
limbs, a belated reaction to the truth. I forced myself to jump
up and walk again.

Of course, the island might be something more than a
private torture chamber. If Dart were brought to trial (that
was how my mind worked), he could possibly provide some

rationale for his "work." Not that any rationale could serve as moral justification for the misery he was inflicting. But it was important to establish just what he was doing, and what were those "three stages" of research of which he had spoken with some pride.

It was not hard to understand how an intelligent man afflicted by his disabilities might be obsessed with the function of those disabilities and their cause. I knew how erroneous was the popular view of scientists as being "detached," of science as being "pure"; scientists, like artists, were often obsessionals, and the most outstanding work came from obsessionals. Dart would have as strong a drive as any man to comprehend the mysteries of genetic structure and programming. *If* that was what he was working on.

So I arrived at the point where I decided that what he was doing might possibly be of value to the world, and that he must immediately be prevented from doing it. Was there a contradiction there? All knowledge was valuable; only in the wrong hands was it destructive, and Dart's were decidedly wrong hands.

If my reasoning was correct, then I had to return and face Dart with greater resolution than I had shown. And more than reason would be required there . . .

So deep in thought was I that I stumbled over a branch half hidden in the grass and fell full length.

Bernie virtually jumped on to me and began patting my hand.

"My Master, good man, good boy. No trouble, no trouble. Take care! You go down, boy, hero, okay!"

"I'm okay," I said, sitting up. "I'm glad of your company, Bernie. Just don't touch me."

The glade we were in was littered with rock and the great white shells of dead tortoises. The sun, high overhead, beat down among the straggling eucalyptus and bamboo. I sat and rubbed my knee, weary again. The swim had been too much. Whatever terrific events may inform our lives, it always comes to that in the end; we just want to lie down.

Leaning back, I shaded my eyes from the sun and watched Bernie cast himself down beside me. The garish distant music came to my ears, together with the continuous sound of the ocean, which one could never escape. I dozed, half comfortable.

A scuffling near at hand brought me back to present realities. Bernie was already peering alertly across my chest at a point to the right.

Only three meters from us, with ponderous tread, a giant tortoise was crossing the clearing. Its head craned on its rough neck, tendons stretching with effort as it pulled at a small plant growing there. It stood for a while, munching the green thing until even the stalk was gone, giving us an abstracted look from its dark liquid eyes. Then it marched past, edging aside the relic of a former comrade as it went. Bernie whined but did not pursue.

So one of the original denizens of the island still managed to survive. For how many millions of years had the giant tortoises had their being on this lonely rock? Looking at that seamed face of a successor to the orders of dinosauria, I had felt time close up between us. Maybe they would flourish here long after humanity was finished. Somewhere beyond these horizons, man was getting ready to extinguish himself.

Directly I thought of that, the problems of Moreau Island became small indeed. Yet the connection between what went on here and what went on *there* did not escape me.

Filled with an unease which at least renewed my energy, I shook Bernie off and rose. Dart was the man I had to deal with.

I went to the gate of the Master's enclosure, Bernie following. The island lay quiet, enjoying its siesta, though the rock music still played.

"Dart!" I called. "Dart!"

After a while, a mechanical-sounding voice near my ear said, "What do you want?"

I looked for the intercom but it was on the inside of the gate, out of harm's way. The arrangement was a good one, considering the deep scratches on the metal of gate and posts.

"Dart, I want you to let me back in. I need to talk to you."

"What do you want to talk about, Mr. Undersecretary? God?"

"I'll settle for lesser subjects—I've been thinking the situation over."

"What situation?"

"There is only one situation on this island, as you know —and you're in it."

Silence.

"And, Dart—I want to bring my pal Bernie along."

Fright showed in the Dog Man's eyes. He understood more than he could express, just like the rest of us.

The gate swung open.

"Come on, Bernie! He won't hurt you! Stay with me."

What a pitiful, divided look I received!

"Master, savvy. You speak. You no drive, Four Long Limbs, no trouble. This my bad house, Lab'raty. No like Whip, be good, be good boy."

He took a step forward and a step back. And another step back.

"You'd better return to the village, then, Bernie. Thanks for coming along."

"Goodbye, good man. One, two, three . . ."

I entered, and the gate closed behind me.

For the first time, I took in the crudity of the construction of the low building. The greatest care had been expended on the front, where the big control room was; there the facade had been given some sort of pebble-dash finish. The rest was roughly done. The walls were of breeze blocks, crudely mortared together; the eaves lacked guttering; and many of the windows were unglazed, the combined effect being one of incompletion if not downright dereliction. One or two tropical creepers, seizing hold of the rough walls, did something to counterbalance the general rawness.

Going through the door into the house, I found Mortimer Dart in the main room, sitting alert in his chair. Again I scrutinized that pale, puffy face, but could read nothing vital. Bella hovered restlessly behind his chair. Heather was in the far corner of the room, sitting by a luxuriant plant in a bronze tub. She wore the same saffron tunic and dark trousers as she had done on our last meeting; to these, she had added a flimsy mauve scarf, which was knotted incongruously round her neck.

I made a small nod in Heather's direction. It was not returned. She remained unmoving.

"A pleasant family gathering," I said. The room was air conditioned. No jingles here; only Haydn played as usual. I shivered.

"You have had a good look round my estate, Roberts."

"Yes. I'm feeling a touch of fever, I believe. Has Bella any more of that lime juice?"

"Of course. Bella! Let me feel your pulse."

I stood there. As he came nearer, the seat of his chair was raised until he was high enough to touch my forehead. The

hand he brought up ended in variegated fingers; the finger he
placed on my forehead was soft and hard at once. I tried to
look at it as the metal hand retracted and hung down again
over the side of the vehicle. Glancing at a small panel of
instruments by his left knee, Dart said, ''Your pulse is normal. Your temperature is a couple of points above average,
but that is only to be expected when you've been walking
about in the sun and swimming in the lagoon. Sit down.''

I guessed I was meant to appreciate his delicate reminder
that he had much of the island under surveillance.

As I sat down, he lowered himself until his eye level was
only slightly above mine, and said, ''I must have your promise not to disrupt the placid routine of what goes on here.
Keep quiet and you are okay. If you upset the Beast People,
or poor Hans, or me, or *anyone*—well, we must take steps.
This is not a fun-fair. You savvy?''

Looking away from him, I asked coldly, ''Have you sent
that radio message yet, Dart?''

''I need certain guarantees—''

''Because you can be in deep trouble if you haven't done
so. Let me remind you forcibly that an extensive Search-
Rescue is under way right now, seeking out survivors from
the *Leda* over an ever widening area of ocean.''

Dart said, ''That was all ten days ago, in the middle of a
war. They'll have packed in the search by now. You can't
kid me.''

''They never give up,'' I said.

Bella came and set a misty glass of lime by my side.

''How is it,'' Dart asked, ''that, if this search you speak
of took place, we've seen no aircraft over the island for more
than a week?''

''That reinforces my point. They have not yet combed this
sector. They'll be around at any time.''

I could see he did not believe me. My discomfort was
added to by private knowledge I had. Ordinarily, survey
satellites high above the stratosphere recorded all land and
ocean activity; one of them would have relayed the sinking
of the *Leda* back to base; but I knew that the vital satellite
had been disintegrated by the enemy only two days previously—the report had come through while I was in conference on the Moon.

Dart began wheeling himself about the room. Bella followed, until he gestured her savagely to get out of the way.

''You have no proof of your identity—'' he began, when

the siren started to blow. He glanced at his watch and said, "We have a punctual computer, you see. That's time to get back to work. End of siesta. End also of our talk."

I put my foot on the footrest of his chair and halted him. "Dart, I demand, as Undersecretary of State, that you or I radio at once to ASASC. Those are my instructions to you, and I must warn you that under the Emergency Powers Act I have the right to commandeer your equipment. If you resist, you can be tried by an emergency court, whose powers include pronouncement of the death sentence. What do you say, Yes or No?"

His face seemed to change shape as he hunched up his shoulders in sudden rage. His hands clasped the arms of his chair.

"The radio transmitter is out of action today," he said at last.

"You're lying!"

"I will not be dictated to on my own island."

"Stay where you are," said a voice from behind.

Turning, I saw the slim man in the white lab coat. He had a withered, dull face, screwed at this moment into an expression of determined nastiness. He held a strange weapon, something like a long air pistol, which he pointed at me.

"Da Silva," I said, "under wartime regulations, you, like your boss, are committing an offense which carries the death penalty. Put that weapon down."

"Okay, Roberts, or whatever your name is, no more bluff."

Dart also had a weapon aimed at me. I recognized it as a Browning automatic. It took little deductive power to realize that he would have a signal device on his chair to summon help when needed.

As I stood there, hands half raised, wondering whether to throw myself on Dart, the other protagonists in the scene were on the move. Bella slunk away, vanishing furtively out of the door like an image of betrayal—though why I expected anything from her I cannot say. By contrast, Heather came closer, rising from her chair and approaching almost as noiselessly as Bella had retreated. At least she was unarmed, but the look on her face was not attractive. A mute signal passed between her and Dart.

"You are recovering your strength and getting dangerous," he said. "We shall have to lock you up. It will give you a chance to think things over."

"You have me at a disadvantage, Dart. That's just temporary as you'll realize if you consider your actions within the context of the war being waged over Pacific waters. You have been informed of my role in affairs. Cooperate, or face the consequences."

Dart kept the weapon leveled at me, smiling thinly. "Warfare . . . the perfect human excuse to exercise power, personal power as well as national. That's your sort of caper, not mine, Mr. Roberts. You think I'm automatically on your side in the struggle, don't you? You're wrong. Humanity always kept me at arm's length; I don't have arms, so I don't have to have human feelings. I'm excused. Okay, savvy?"

"It's not a matter of what you feel—"

"That'll do, thanks a lot. Da Silva, lock him up."

6

A Little Striptease

To estimate the size of the building over which Dart's will prevailed was not easy.

From outside, it was almost impossible, for the structure had been sited so that it backed on to the thickly afforested hill which ran up toward the eastern end of the island. In addition, it was surrounded by the high stockade.

From inside, locked doors foiled any attempts at exploration. I knew only two corridors, which formed a T, and some of the rooms off them. On one side of the longer corridor were the rooms whose windows faced out over what I suppose served as the front of the building. These rooms consisted of two cell-like bedrooms, in one of which I had been lodged when I first arrived, another small room with a locked door, and the large control room. These rooms faced northwest. On the other side of the corridor were the kitchen, Bella's room, a generator room (locked), then the side corridor, then a store, a hall with double doors (locked) to the laboratory area, and a W.C. Down the side corridor were more locked doors, Dart's quarters, Heather's quarters, toilets, and, I suspected, the radio room, as well as another locked door to the labs. I estimated that the T-corridors gave access to less than a third of the total building.

Under surveillance of the two guns, I was taken to a cell next to the generator room and locked in. There was a light in the cell and a vent in the ceiling. I judged from its position in the house that it was entirely surrounded by other rooms, perhaps other cells. It contained a bunk with two blankets and a paperback novel on it, and a slop pail standing in one corner. Nothing else.

Burning with fury and frustration, I marched up and down the tiny room.

A long time passed. Hours uncounted. Then the door was unlocked. Heather came in warily with a tray of food. Da Silva stood behind her, still carrying his air pistol. She put the tray down on the floor and left. The key turned in the lock.

Long after that, I fell on the bunk and went to sleep. When I woke, the light still glared down into my eyes. I had no idea whether it was night or day.

Never in my life had I been held prisoner. It was impossible to recapture the sustaining rage I had felt when first shut in. I began pacing again, but this time it was to keep anxieties at bay.

Heather returned and took the tray away. I had eaten nothing. She was back fairly soon, with more food and a cup of hot coffee. As soon as she had gone, I squatted down and drank the coffee avidly. I ate the food. I began to pace again.

Long after I had wearied of pacing, and was sitting sprawled on the bunk, there was a thump on the door.

"Mr. Roberts? It's me, Mortimer Dart. I expect you can hear? I've come to say that everything's okay and that we're going to let you out. You hear me?"

I remained on the bed. A trick? Were they going to shoot me? What had they to lose?

"Mr. Roberts, are you awake? Don't try anything. You're free to go and I don't want any trouble. We've checked on your credentials and you're genuine. I'm convinced."

"You checked with ASASC?" I asked.

A small silence. Then he said, "I was suspicious with good reason. No mention of you being missing on the Co-Allied News. So I couldn't believe your story. You had no verification, did you? How did I know you weren't some sort of a subversive?"

"Dart, *did you check with ASASC?*"

"It was on the news this morning, Mr. Roberts. You know

how they censor things in wartime. They flashed your picture and announced you just died in a Washington hospital. Your funeral is three tomorrow afternoon. That's interesting, isn't it?''

So they had given up the search. The cover story was characteristic; the public did not like to hear that politicians went on risky missions. But—did Dart know that? Did he still have doubts about my identity? If he did believe I was a subversive, he would have reason to kill me. On the other hand, if he did now believe that I was who I claimed to be, he would still have good reason for not wanting my return to the States.

"You hear what I say in there? If I let you out, can I count on your cooperation? No funny business?"

He had not radioed ASASC. That alone was proof I had good reason for mistrust. It was essential that I humor him, at least until I was as far from this cell as I could get.

"Let me out," I said. "Maybe we can watch my funeral on 3V together."

Relief sounded in his voice as he said, "Maybe we can. Quite a giggle. Meanwhile, I have a little trouble on my hands and I might be glad of your help, if you feel so inclined."

The key turned in the lock. The door opened. He was clad in his amazing prosthetic armor, looking as he had done when I first encountered him, robot-like, his helmet almost brushing the ceiling. Despite myself, I was caught off guard. I sidled cautiously past into the corridor. Heather was standing there; she flashed me a strained smile.

I looked up at Dart, at a psychological disadvantage after my period of confinement. The time would come when he would regret his treatment of me.

He said coldly, "So, how does it feel to be dead and practically buried?"

"All right, Dart, you know I'm alive because you need my help. I'll decide about that when I hear what your trouble is. Been whipping Bella again?"

"It's Hans," Heather said.

"He's drunk again," Dart said.

"He's gone on strike," she said quickly.

I looked from one to the other, conscious that I had them momentarily at a small disadvantage.

"Get your stories straight. What *is* Maastricht's trouble?"

"He thought it was a mistake to lock you up," Heather

said, with a defiance in her tone which I guessed must be aimed at Dart. "So he deliberately hit the bottle."

Dart said, "I have to go out there. The Beasts will not work. I would be grateful if you would come along. Just to show yourself in the village. I think they should be put in the picture and see that you are okay."

"Where's Maastricht?"

"He's out there. Come with me, Roberts. We'll get him back here. There's no danger."

"That's not the impression I get from you. What time is it?"

"Three-thirty in the afternoon."

I had been in the cell for some twenty-five hours.

We moved down the corridor, the Master clomping heavily along, Heather light and tricky beside him. Mad thoughts ran through my brain; the freedom from the cell brought an unexpected agoraphobia. We reached the door at the far end of the corridor and went outside into the compound. I breathed deep of the warm air. It smelled good. It promised freedom.

Heather let us out of the gate and we stood there under the trees, taking in the scene, as the dull eternal boom of ocean met us.

My eyes went first to the stretch of open sea. It was empty. And there were no planes in the sky; it too was empty. War gave no sign.

The scene on land was almost as null and void. Across the lagoon, I could see a few shadowy figures lying outside their huts. Nobody was stirring. Nearer at hand, the crane stood. In the intense clear light, I could see Maastricht sprawling in the open cab. Outside, leaning against the crane's tracks, was Maastricht's hulking friend George, his leather hat tipped over his eyes and his arms folded, looking completely human in that attitude from this distance.

"It all looks peaceful and harmless," I said. "Let well alone, Dart. If Hans has had a drop too much, let him sleep it off."

"Discipline, Mr. Roberts. You in your profession must know the importance of discipline."

He had a radio amplifier fitted into the breastplate of his armor. Swiveling out a hand mike, he spoke into it. "Hans, snap out of it! Get cracking. Stir it up, will you? Out, everyone, work, work! The Master's is the Wrath that Flames. The Master's is the Whip that Tames."

There was an immediate stir among the tawdry huts, as the amplified voice went booming across the island. On Maastricht, too, the noise had the desired effect.

I saw Hans stagger to his feet and peer across to where we stood. He rubbed his face, came to the step of the cab, and practically fell to the ground. George jumped up in panic to scuttle to his aid—whereupon Maastricht picked himself up, gave his unlucky foreman a blow in the chest, and started yelling at him.

With a shrill whistle, George went into action. He started running around the crescent of the lagoon at an amazing pace, waving his arms, bellowing. It was an odd sight, partly saddening, partly funny.

What was partly funny developed into a more broadly humorous scene. As George neared the village with all the ostentation of a traction engine, a man came trotting out from the trees in the opposite direction, running along the path I had taken on my arrival here. This newcomer was sturdy and very red, with a fuzz of hair standing out over his brow and a snipy snout. Although he wore a pair of the universal coveralls, he had snipped the legs off to reveal his long shanks, as if he was proud to look more human in that respect than most of his fellows. I have called him a man, but he was only manlike. He resembled those foxes in children's books who dress in men's clothes for purposes of deception.

He was moving fast. He and George both swerved to avoid each other. But they both swerved in the same direction and so collided just the same. They fell over, rolled about, and immediately began to fight.

Maastricht's drunken laughter echoed across the lagoon.

"We must break that up!" said Dart. "This is not a fun-fair."

He raised his carbine and fired it into the air, twice.

As soon as the fight commenced, the Beast People began rushing toward the action. The shots halted them momentarily. Then their curiosity got the better of them, and they dashed forward again. With a cry of anger, the cyborg started toward them, moving rapidly on his power-assisted legs. I followed more slowly, walking down the shadow-flecked path until I was halfway between the fight and the point on the harbor where Maastricht stood, still laughing inanely.

The arrival of the Master on the scene was sufficient for

the Beast People. They broke and ran, jumping among the bushes and huts with no regard for any scratches they might receive. Even George and Foxy broke apart, to stand glaring at each other and breathing heavily.

Both creatures were bleeding freely, as I saw when I got closer. Foxy nursed his left arm. The sleeve was torn away, revealing a long tear in the sandy flesh where George's teeth had slashed. George had the heavier build and did not seem hurt, although his lower lip was swollen and leaked blood which he did not attempt to stanch. They held their ground and glared defiance, at Dart as well as at each other.

Dart—wisely, I thought—said in calmer tones, "Okay, back to work, everyone! George, get back to the crane. Do what I say, no cause trouble." He drew his whip and cracked it.

"I all kill up boss-man George very soon," Foxy said distinctly. He got the whip across his shoulders and fled.

In contrast with the sullen submission I had seen so far, Foxy's was an exceptional piece of defiance—and couched in exceptionally clear English. Maybe the Master thought so as well; but he contented himself by shouting a threat at Foxy's retreating back before stomping off toward the crane.

George, muttering darkly to himself, cast about on the ground, picked up his dusty hat, and rammed it on his head. As if in so doing he regained his courage, he went galloping off toward the harbor, overtaking the Master, waving his stubby arms and yowling, much as he had done previously.

I stood in the shade of a tree, watching, certain that there would be trouble between Dart and Maastricht. The latter was too drunk at present; but later he might be a valuable ally against Dart. The two of us would be more than a match for Dart, for all his armament, if we stayed outside the compound. And Maastricht had a carbine.

Maastricht stopped laughing as Dart approached and began shouting instead. Dart shouted back. A slanging match developed. I saw Dart stoop and seize Maastricht's half-empty bottle from where it stood on top of the caterpillar track. He flung it out toward the open sea.

Uttering a few curses, Maastricht climbed awkwardly into the crane and started it up. George set up a loud hullabaloo. The workers were running past where I stood, jostling to get back to their rocks and their cement. Satisfied, Dart turned away. I walked forward.

Maastricht started up the crane. It began to crawl slowly

along the harbor edge. He leaned out of the cab to shout to George, who was furiously conducting the workers. As he did so, he caught my eye, and raised a thumb in a gesture of defiance to the fates. I signaled back. And at that moment the crane tipped forward.

I saw the far track go over the edge of the concrete in a shower of mortar. Slowly, the machine canted to one side. Maastricht swore, tugging at a lever. Its engine roared and the track spun. Then the whole thing slewed over and plunged into the lagoon.

I yelled and broke into a run.

The scene was one of tremendous confusion.

The Beast People milled about on the edge of the water, uttering a medley of cries. Most of them appeared in genuine terror—though here and there I saw furtive gloating at the disaster. Many plunged to the edge of the water, jumping on the rocks and collapsed cement wall without daring to venture into the alien element. One old fellow with a face like a horse fell in; in the scramble to rescue him, others joined him in the water. Never was there so much screaming and crying!

And George—he was the most demented! He charged madly to and fro, hooting madly. Finally, he flung himself in the lagoon and was forced to scramble out again at once.

All this was marginal to my attention. My eyes were fixed on the great confusion in the water where the crane had gone down. One corner of the cab and a section of track was above water. Bubbles came billowing up. There was no sign of Maastricht. I kicked my shoes off.

"Roberts, please—please save him!"

I heard Dart's words as I dived in.

On the first dive I found Hans. Slicing under the cab, kicking strongly in the muddied water, I came on his naked back and right leg. He was struggling. A great deal of sand and muck had been churned up, but I saw that his arms had in some way been trapped in the entrance of the cab and were wedged from inside. His head was in the cab, the rest of him outside, as though he had almost been flung out as the machine tipped over. I seized and shook his shoulder to let him know that help was on the way before returning to the surface to regain breath.

I went down again through the upper door of the cab, plunging down to him through the clouded water. Diesel oil seeped up past my eyes.

Maastricht's face was close to mine, full of anguish. His carbine and its strap had caught in the grip by the door, trapping his arm as he had tried to jump free. His left arm was still fighting to release himself. It took me only a moment to push the weapon out of the way and let his arm go. I seized him under the armpits and heaved at him.

What I needed was more purchase. For that, I had to get further through the cab and grasp his torso. Against myself, I was forced up to the surface.

Those dark and alien faces whirled round me. What a racket they made—or else it was the blood hammering in my arteries. Dizzily, I gulped air, then plunged for the third time, right down through the cab.

This time, I got my arms round Hans and my feet against the caterpillar wheels. I heaved and tugged and slipped. He was still struggling. Still I could not budge him. With my head in the murk and a vague square shadow of light above me, I heaved . . . and heaved again, unable to understand why he did not now float free. With my lungs bursting, I kicked down further and found that his left leg was pinned between crane and lagoon floor.

When I returned to the world of sunlight, the Master loomed above me on the broken wall.

"Get him up, you must get him up, Cal!"

George was up to his hocks in the water, his black gaze devouring me. "You fish me out water—please!" Much later, reviewing the scene, recalling what George had said as he crouched there with his great neckless head thrust forward, I asked myself, *Just a confusion with pronouns or a genuine identification with the drowning man?*

But the one creature there with real presence of mind was Foxy. He pushed through the melee with a length of rope from the building site. He threw one end to me, with a curious glance of triumph and mistrust from his shifty red eyes.

"Take the other end, Dart," I called. Then I dived once more.

It was no problem to tie the rope about Hans' chest. His eyes still stared, his hair streamed upward, tendrils of his beard drifted into his open mouth. Slithering in the muck on the floor of the lagoon, I jerked on the rope and kicked out for the surface.

Dart heaved at the rope. The rabble, despite their awe of him, also pulled. It was a ghastly tug-of-war, during which I

had visions of Hans floating up with one leg missing. But he
never floated up at all.

Twice more I dived to the lagoon floor. His leg and foot
were crushed between the crane and one of the slabs of rock
thrown in to build the harbor.

At last I pulled myself out of the water.

"He's trapped. You're going to have to move the crane,"
I told Dart. "Harness up the two landing craft with hawsers.
If you can shift it a few inches, Hans will come free. Speed
it up!"

They did as I suggested. The operation was a shambles.
What should have taken ten minutes, not more, took over an
hour. Eventually, the crane was got to move, and we hauled
poor Hans up. Dart laid about him with the whip while I
applied the kiss of life. No response.

We emptied a gallon of water out of his lungs and I tried
again. It did not work. Hans Maastricht was dead.

I squatted by his pale body, looking round at those who
had known him. I was getting to recognize many individuals;
not merely George, giving me his black inscrutable stare,
Bernie, pleasingly staying as near as he could, Foxy, sneer-
ing over some secret pleasure, but several others—an old
gray Swine Woman, a heavy Horse-Hippo with slow tread,
a pair of Bull Men, very morose. They had enjoyed the
excitement; most of them were beginning to back away, content to leave the sprawled body where it lay.

Dart pointed his whip at the two Bull Men. "You two—
carry the body to HQ. Pick it up. Quickly!"

They seized Hans' body by the shoulders, dragging it
slowly along without expression beyond a habitual one of
grievance, letting the dead man's heels trail along the
ground. Dart strode on ahead. George trotted about beside
the Bull Men, patting the body, prodding it, as if unable to
believe that life had fled. The rest of the Beast People milled
about and started to trail home. Foxy had disappeared.

The body was brought to a small surgery in one corner of
the laboratory block. This was the first time I had been here;
something of the Bull Men's unease communicated itself to
me. When the corpse was laid on a table, Dart shooed the
carriers outside.

"Come back tomorrow. Tomorrow funeral—bury Hans,
savvy? Hans go underground, meet Big Master. Savvy?"

The Bull Men looked gloomily at me. Then they turned
and galloped for the exit. Dart locked the gate behind them

and we went indoors. I got a towel from my bedroom and dried myself.

When he appeared in the doorway, Dart had shed his armor and was back in the chair.

"This is a miserable turn of events, to be sure! Well, that's what life's all about. Always some fresh misery."

"I notice you try to inculcate religion into your people, even if you don't believe in God yourself!"

"You can cook without eating the food yourself. You mean that business about 'Big Master underground'? We'll have more of that at the funeral tomorrow—which we'll hold at three p.m., the same time as your fictitious funeral. There's bloody hypocrisy—but you didn't object to that, did you?"

"Hans is unmistakably dead. At least give him a proper burial."

"It's a good chance to rub in the Big Master stuff. It does no harm—it's designed to keep them in order, to worry them that someone invisible with an even bigger whip than mine might be watching them when I'm not about. Isn't that how all religions started?"

"You're bitter about your country, your name, your religion—I can see you have your reasons, but, after all this while, can't you come to terms with your disabilities? You've done well in that respect physically; why cripple yourself spiritually?"

He gave a cold smile. "If I believed in your bloody Christian God, then I'd have to believe that he made me in his image. Neither you nor I would want a God who looked like that, so that's all there is about it. Now, give up trying to rile me. Enough's enough for one day. Come and have a whisky with me, like a man. A sundowner."

"A cordial will do me."

Bella brought us in two plastic trays of lunch and we ate together in the control room, with Bella leaning behind Dart's chair. I gathered she ate in whatever served as the kitchen. Looking at her, I shuddered; the mixture of woman and beast in her seemed so complex; in her slinking attitude was something seductive, yet her face was terrifyingly ugly under its dark wig.

In the manner of one making conversation, Dart said, "A little drink does a man no harm. It's a custom that goes with civilization. Too much drink is another matter; you lose control. That was poor Hans' trouble. His grandmother was a Malay. He drank too much and today it finished him off.''

"No. He may have drunk too much, but what finished him off was the rotten way the harbor was built. The concrete collapsed.''

"He was boozed and drove over the side.''

"Not so! The wall collapsed and the crane tipped over. It wasn't Hans' fault. The lousy setup here on Moreau Island killed him.''

"It was drink, I tell you—I've known Hans for years. He had colored blood in him. I always said booze would kill him.''

I grew angry. "What if booze *did* kill the poor guy? Why did he take to the bottle? Just to blot out the shame of living here with these mutilated creatures, these parodies of human beings.''

Looking down at his plate, Dart said, "I knew him best. You don't understand, Roberts. You're only a bloody politician. I was fond of Hans. I'm going to miss him. . . . Oh, confound the whole damned rotten human setup!'' He struck the table with a metal fist. The violence of the gesture soothed him. He looked up at me and said, in a perfectly calm manner, "We were on good terms, Hans and me. He had had a rough deal from life, right since he was a kid. This island was a sanctuary for him—for once he wasn't on the receiving end. So he understood how I felt and I understood how he felt. Now you and I . . .''

He let the sentence hang there. When I refused to say anything, he started again.

"You and I—could we ever be on good terms? You're a man of power, you've been around, you are probably on good terms with everyone you meet. You don't even know what 'good terms' means—it's something you take for granted. I can never have that relationship because of what I am. A thalidomide freak. I have to rule or go under. Does that sound like megalomania to you? Well, it's not. It's the result of experience, and you don't buck experience. Not that I've any ideas about ruling anything but this little blob in the ocean—that's all I want. But I don't know what you're thinking, do I? For all I know, you're thinking you ought to wipe me out.''

I looked out of the window.

"I don't think in those terms. I can see you are determined

to force me into opposition to you, whether you realize it or not, but that's a result of your paranoia, not my behavior."

"My paranoia! What old cant are you handing me? Do you know—have you any idea what paranoia is? It's a rational reaction to surrounding circumstances. Why shouldn't you be thinking about wiping me out? There's a war going on all around the world, which you're part of and I'm not. Who's fighting that war, ask yourself! Not freaks like me, Mr. Roberts, no, but normals like you! War's your idea! Wiping out's your idea."

He was trembling now, and I could feel anger rising in me.

"You aren't exempt from guilt, Dart. Listen to what you're saying. You're talking to me as if I were a multitude, not an individual. You know very well war was not my idea, but if you can see me as a force rather than a person, then it's easier for you to hate me. That's how wars begin. Your deformities don't give you any monopoly over right."

In speaking, I was leaning forward, pointing a finger at him. He seized on the gesture and starting shouting before I could finish.

"I don't want to hear your crap! Take a look at yourself! You are instinctively aiming a gun at me now, only all you have is a finger. So watch it, because I am armed, remember!"

He brought up the automatic and aimed it at my stomach.

"Now who's thinking about wiping out?" I asked. "You're right, Dart—only when you've got that thing in your claw can you be on equal terms with another man. I wonder you dared let poor Maastricht carry a gun."

Although he remained pointing the gun at me, his gaze left mine. He gazed down at the floor with little darting glances and began to bite on his lower lip.

When he looked up at me again, he put the automatic back in a clip on the inside of his chair, and said, "I have a hasty temper, Mr. Roberts, and you deliberately tried making me shirty. All I was trying to tell you was that I wanted us to be on good terms. I want you to do something for me. I've just remembered that we haven't got Hans' carbine. Where is it? Down on the bed of the lagoon?"

"It's safe there. The Beast People don't dare enter the water."

"You must get that gun for me, Mr. Roberts. If you don't, they will." He hitched himself up in the chair in agitation.

"They mustn't have firearms. Try and imagine the havoc they'd cause."

"I'm not going diving again, Dart, that's final. You saw George and the rest of them. They are afraid of water."

"It's the Seal People, Roberts. The Seal People! They'll dive down and get the carbine. They might give it to the villagers, to Foxy, or one of the others. They're all in league together. We'd have a full-scale uprising on our hands. Will you please go and get that gun—now, before sunset."

Privately, I doubted whether the seals would be able to find the carbine, even if they went looking for it. I shook my head, waiting to see if Dart would draw his gun on me again. Instead, he pressed a button on his chair arm.

Bella appeared.

"Fetch Heather here," Dart commanded.

He gave me as unpleasant a smile as I had ever seen but remained silent.

In a minute, Bella returned with the dark American girl. She walked springily over to Dart's side and stood there attentively, nibbling an index finger. Bella stood behind me, by the door.

"Heather is a remarkable young lady, Mr. Roberts. My admiration of her is almost unbounded. She is very kind and very beautiful. Heather, my pet, would you kindly remove your clothes so that Mr. Roberts can see how beautiful you are? Bella, put a light on."

Heather was wearing the same costume she had worn earlier. She moved to one side so that she had plenty of room; and then she began to undress. She bent and removed her sandals, placing them together. Smiling remotely at me, she set her head on one side and unknotted the incongruous scarf. She pulled it from her neck and, extending her arm, let the material float to the floor. It was clear that she was expert at provocation. Next, she slowly undid the buttons of her saffron tunic, working from collarbone to navel, until the garment opened, revealing the flesh beneath it. With delicacy, she peeled the tunic from her narrow shoulders, casting it to the floor over the scarf, shaking her hair free as she did so. The movement emphasized the beauty of her breasts, which were not particularly full; she caressed the left one with her hand, running one of the nipples between her fingers as she did so.

A furtive movement elsewhere caught my eye. Bella was slinking from the room.

Now Heather walked round the pile of her clothes in a circle, maybe to emphasize the springiness of her breasts. Then she paused, facing us again, and began meditatively to unzip her trousers. She undid a hook at the top and they fell about her knees. She wore nothing underneath them. As she bent to pick the trousers up, I was given a glimpse of perfect buttocks and thighs. When she turned to face us again, her cheeks slightly flushed, the smile slightly more lascivious, the dark hair on her mons veneris was invitingly revealed. She came two steps nearer to me before covering it slyly with both hands. She ran her tongue across her lips, then suddenly threw up her arms and ran to the other end of the room.

"Thank you, Heather," Dart said, his voice thick. "You would be happy to spend the night with Mr. Roberts if he did me a little favor, wouldn't you?"

"It would be a pleasure," she said. "Wouldn't it, Calvert?"

Dart said, "It's time we were more hospitable to you, Mr. Roberts. But first, please, that carbine."

"You're up to your old tricks, Dart—you are using us both as your objects. Like I said, no dice. Thanks for the strip-tease, Heather. You should develop it—and get a better job elsewhere."

"Men who attain positions of power frequently do so by suppressing their sexual drive," Dart said, flatly. He added after a moment, "That's what you call a tradeoff . . ."

Outside, darkness had fallen. The ocean, beyond which war lived and thrived, was no longer visible. Only its sound could be heard, like continuous cannon.

7

The Funeral Was Well Attended

When dawn came, I was praying.

I still clung, despairingly perhaps, to a belief in the idea of a God. The conception of a deity who was judge between good and evil was fundamental. In good and evil I did still believe, seeing them at war in society and in individuals every day of my life, and it made sense for men to worship anything that would help fortify the good in their natures. But that was an act of intellect, not faith. Such was my religion.

The expediency of war had blurred many issues, but Mortimer Dart served to remind me that basically I saw human existence as I had when a boy—a battle between good and evil. In the present war, the country I loved and served stood for the good.

Dart was an instance of how circumstances could mold human nature for the worst. He might have started as pitiably as Frankenstein's monster; but he had turned himself into a Frankenstein—a victor, not a victim.

He had to be rendered harmless. Yet the harm he did here was nothing compared with the harm being done in the world beyond the island.

But to remove Dart—and the seductive Heather—like a

bad tooth. That would leave the island without control. I foresaw a general bloodbath, with the Beast People slaughtering each other wholesale. It would be best to gain control of the island and then summon help.

My duty was to return to work as soon as possible. But I had duties here too; I could not just seize a landing craft and set off with a compass into the wide blue yonder.

These meditations made me gloomy but determined, and it was in that mood that I ate breakfast when Bella brought it in.

"Shall you go to Hans' funeral, Bella?"

"Master bury Hans, dig in ground. Hans no more need air, go bury in ground."

"It will happen to us all, Bella."

The blank feline stare came then, and the wrinkled brow under the wig. I thought that if Dart were trying to create animals in the image of men, that he should perhaps start from the inside, not the outside. Could Bella ever comprehend that one day she also would need air no more?

She was human enough to lock the door after she left. Maybe Dart was right; any guy who could resist the seductions of Heather should not be trusted. . . .

I sat tight and was released after lunch. The Master had a weakness. He needed me. Da Silva drove up an antique American army truck from somewhere round the back of the premises and left it in the shade, close to piles of old lumber and gallon cans of paint. In the back of the truck lay a wooden coffin. A branch of hibiscus had been thrown across it. As I stood sunning myself, Heather appeared on the step.

She called out, "Hi, how are you this afternoon?"

Walking over to her, I asked where Dart was.

"You don't think I'm waiting for Warren, do you? The Master will be along when he's good and ready."

"I'm sorry that he made you strip for me yesterday."

"Don't make me laugh! I enjoyed it, and you did too, or else what kind of a guy are you? There are few enough men to strip to here, that's for sure. Come on, say you liked it!"

"You have a gorgeous body, Heather, but the performance demeaned us all. We're not animals."

After a small silence, I said, "I've heard Warren mentioned before. Exactly who is this elusive fellow Warren? Does he live hereabouts?"

"We're not supposed to say anything about Warren. Relax, he isn't here." She slid her arm through mine.

"What's the matter with you, Cal? You were making come-hither remarks to me the first time we met."

I laughed. "And you were telling me to keep my distance."

"Put your hand down here, between my legs." She rubbed against me and I felt myself stirring. Hating myself for it, I moved off.

"How much provocation do you need, Cal?" she asked, eyes glittering in the sun.

She was stretching out to me again when the Master appeared. He was walking tall, dressed in his prosthetic armor. Certainly he made a formidable sight, clumping across the courtyard, riot gun slung across his shoulder, whip tucked into his belt.

"Mr. Roberts, you ready for the burial? I can see Hans is. Climb in beside me. Wait—you drive—it'll be easier for you than for me. I'll show you which way to go. Heather, you stay here."

She was already climbing into the vehicle. "Hey, I'm coming with you! I want to see the fun. I like hearing the animals do their thing. You said I could come along."

"Sorry, pet. This is an occasion when the animals get a little instruction, and they won't listen if they've got you to goggle at. Besides, I don't want to leave Bella alone in the house. Down you get."

Heather looked mutinous for a moment. Then she climbed down.

"Fuck you, Mort," she said.

"Open up the gate and let us through," he said. "And don't be common."

She did as instructed. I rolled the vehicle forward, and the gate closed behind us.

"We bury the coffin up the hill," Dart said. "But first we go round to the village and rouse everyone up. Just to put you in the picture, this is a big event on Moreau Island."

"Where did you get Heather from, Dart?"

"Heather's here voluntarily, believe it or not. She opted for the life. A private plane made a forced landing here at the beginning of the war, fleeing from the invasion of Samoa by the Cubans. She decided this was the refuge she was looking for. It's as simple as that."

We took the primitive road to the village and I drew up where Dart instructed me, before the first shacks.

The Beast People were already on the move, even before

he stood up in the truck and started shouting at them. It was no longer a shock to see their hideous variety as they shambled forth, dressed in ungainly coveralls, the females adorned with bones and shells festooned about their necks or in their hair. The pair of Bull Men came shuffling out, closely tagged by a Cat Woman who slightly resembled Bella. And there was a Swine Woman with hideous visage and plodding gait, and a bushy creature like a bear, and two small Bear Beings, who frisked and were quite appealing, and ape-like people, and many more, bringing themselves out into the light of day at the sound of their Master's voice.

The stubbly-faced George rushed forward, pushing the others aside with his thick shoulders hunched, snorting as he came. My friend Bernie ran beside him, glancing ever eagerly up at his boar-jackal companion. When he saw me, Bernie ran to my side of the truck, panting his name, panting my name, and then running back to George. Then he came to me again, but could not stay, and ran once more to George, totally undecided.

"This day big holiday, savvy!" the Master shouted to them. "Your friend Hans, he break Law, he get bottle, he finished. You people savvy finished. *Kaput*. All done. Today big funeral. You all come along me, bury Hans in Death Place. Hans with bottle, he go underground, meet Big Master. Come on now, quick time. Obey the Law, follow my car."

While he was shouting variations on this theme, I saw that ginger Foxy was emerging from among the trees. His shanks were bare, as on the day before, but today he further distinguished himself from the crowd by wearing a long shoddy cape over his lean shoulders. As he slunk forward, keeping warily behind the gray Horse-Hippo, I was reminded again of countless children's stories in which wolves and foxes, dressed in human clothes, played the villain. None did it better than Foxy, or looked more disreputable.

Dart saw him and called to him. "Foxy, you and George get all people to the Death Place, savvy? Follow along my car."

Dozens of loaded eyes watched as I reversed the truck and drove it slowly back the way we had come. I caught snatches of their furtive talk as they followed close. They were curious about me; the legend of my having been dragged out of the sea made them unsure whether I was completely human.

As we moved at funeral pace, a large ape-man took hold of the truck and strode along beside me. Although his body closely resembled a gorilla's, his face was completely malformed and, with its long snout, resembled a tapir's as much as anything.

Mortimer Dart glanced at him in approval.

"That's Alpha, helping you along. His brother Beta's just behind. You're growing used to them now, Roberts, aren't you? I told you my experiments here have gone through three stages. Alpha and Beta belong to the second stage, which I have now abandoned as just not on. He's not the result of mere crude vivisection, as in McMoreau's day. He's a product of genetic surgery. Of course, he was of McMoreau stock—that's the reason why we keep the village thriving, for the laboratory. By working on actual genetic material, I was able to alter his entire skull formation."

"Don't expect admiration from me."

"It's quite a trick—it deserves admiration, believe you me. Unfortunately, Alpha has almost no brain, as X-rays show. He just about knows enough to stuff his face with food twice a day. But he was a step in the right direction."

We had passed the head of the lagoon now, and Dart directed me to drive past the palisade to where the road began sloping upward to higher ground. I could see how extensive the Master's headquarters were. The outer wall was so high, and so protected by trees, that we could not make out more than the roofs of the buildings.

I had to keep my eye on the road, which became more difficult to negotiate as it grew steeper. It was littered with stones and chunks of rock, and soon almost ceased to be a road. Soon we were driving over naked rock, across which frequent fissures ran. The vegetation, having to deal with the same obdurate rock, grew lower as it closed in on us. Alpha, the ape-man, fell behind as he was raked by broad thorny leaves.

"The next is the sticky bit," Dart said. I took a quick glance at him. I could see that the jolting was making him suffer inside his armor.

I engaged four-wheel drive as the rock humped itself, and took the stretch ahead as fast as I could. We bumped over a succession of roots like fossil snakes, swerved to miss a gigantic coconut palm, and then followed the trail as it curved and climbed to the left. The back wheels spun and then we were up on a small plateau in a shower of dirt.

"Just ahead past that rattan thicket," Dart said.

A great bird crashed off through the branches above us as I followed what path there was. When we were through the little grove, I braked, stopped the engine, and climbed down. This was the Death Place.

Our burst of speed had set the Beast People some way behind. I left Dart gasping in his seat and went to look round. A patch of ground had been roughly cleared; several slabs of rock stood from the ground, memorials to the dead. Below, scarcely glimpsed through scrub and jungle, was the section of the island I knew. On the other side was the unknown half. It hardly looked inviting. The land rose brokenly, covered in thick vegetation.

Something lay gleaming on the far side of the crude cemetery. I walked among the rocks and pushed through thick feathery grass, growing from pebbles. Things scuttled and slithered under my feet; I kept a watch for snakes but saw only harmless green lizards.

A gigantic metal framework lay among the undergrowth, almost smothered in vegetation. I traced it along as best I could, until a thorn thicket stopped me. I followed it in the opposite direction, but the end went over a precipitous gully where I could not follow, and was lost among low trees. It looked like a gigantic pylon of some kind. I turned back to the truck. Dart switched on a cassette player and savage music started and a roaring voice sang.

> Animal or human, cast an eye
> On the mystery of Death and Birth—
> The Shape you're given the day you're born
> Is lost when we put you under earth.
>
> So human or animal, take good care
> To speak with speech and obey the Creed—
> It's better to suffer and keep your Shape
> Than lose it all and be dead indeed.
>
> Animal or human or human-like,
> The Master watches you and you know why—
> For when we put you under earth
> You meet the bigger Master in the Sky,
> With a bigger Whip and a bigger trip—
> That Master in the Sky!

"How do you like it?" Dart asked, when I reached the truck. "I wrote it myself. The tune's an old English traditional air. It's the nearest I'll ever get to a hymn. The beasts like it because the words are simple and the sentiment's memorable."

I recognized Dart as the singer. He had enlisted the aid of a synthesizer, and deepened and enriched his slightly reedy tenor.

"We get the Creed later," he said. "The Beast People really go for that—you'll hear. You see, one thing I could have been if my life had been normal was a songwriter. I had a flair for it. You probably heard my jingles in the village, 'Be Beastly Now,' and so on and so forth."

"This hymn of yours sets you up as a sort of God. It's cheap blasphemy."

He looked ugly, and was evidently still in pain from the drive. "No, Roberts, not cheap—dear. Everything I've got I've bought dear. In the Creed, I set myself up as the ideal standard of beauty on this dump. Why not? If everyone had limbs like mine, that would be the measure of beauty, right?"

Dart laughed. I looked beyond him, listening to the ever present boom of the ocean against rock, and tracing with my eye the huge metal structure, couched among the undergrowth like the carcass of a giant animal.

"Dart?"

He was recovered, although the sweat glittered on his forehead under the helmet.

"What's the pylon object lying in the undergrowth back there?"

"It *is* a pylon. Dates from the eighties and the old Omega global navigational system. Cost billions of dollars and was obsolete as soon as erected. The world's a sideshow really —don't even you sometimes feel that?"

"Frankly, no."

"That's what I like about you, Mr. Roberts—you're always good for a spot of conversation."

The Beast People were filling the clearing now, shambling up and gathering round the perimeters of the cemetery, glancing at each other meanwhile, unclear of their roles. The effect was stunningly like a human gathering at a burial when, if ever, daily functions catch us unrehearsed for the presence of death. These uncouth and ailing parishioners had most things in common with my own kind, and I felt my mistrust of them diminish.

While the Master supervised four of them in digging a grave with some entrenching tools, courtesy of U.S. Army, which he had brought along, I took a closer look at the slabs of rock that served as gravestone. They numbered seven. Four of them had names cut, or rather scratched, in their surface; Jimmy Baedermeyer, Chuck Hapgood, Ed Bergetti, Andy Hall. Beneath each name was their year of death—the same year in all cases—below that the letters "R.I.P.," and below that, faintly scratched, the initials "H.M." Hans—he had taken the trouble to commemorate the dead. I wondered if the four men had any connection with the private plane which, according to Dart, had brought Heather here from Samoa.

Dart glanced at the watch plugged into his cyborg arm.

"Getting on for three o'clock, Mr. Roberts. Of course, there's a difference of time zones, but I like to think that your high-up chums in Washington are holding a funeral for you right now. Full religious rites and all that, faces as long as your sleeve. . . . Which ceremony is the bigger fake, do you reckon?"

"You told me you cared for Hans."

He grunted dismissively. "Do you think I care for his corpse? Do you think *he* does? . . . Wait till this lot get worked up in a bit. You'll enjoy it. There's more genuine feeling running here than in Washington, I promise you that."

I wiped sweat from my forehead. "Aren't you a bit afraid of them?"

After a moment's silence, during which he stared out at the Beast People, he said, in a more serious tone than he had been using, "In a way, I regard them as my kind. None of us belong anywhere but on Moreau Island . . ."

Maybe he thought these covert pleas for sympathy had some effect on me.

The hole for Maastricht's coffin was dug with great effort. Even the brawniest of the Beast People were making slow headway. Finally, Dart cried, "That'll do! We aren't trying to strike oil. George, Alpha, help get the coffin off the truck, and go easy with it. If you drop it, you go in the hole yourself."

I watched him closely. He never kept still, striding mechanically from side to side, flicking the whip, and towering over the submissive and unkempt heads of the Beast People.

The hole was less than a meter deep. As he passed me, I said, "Are you down to the rock? It's a very shallow grave."

"I wouldn't put it past them to try and dig Hans up once we're gone, would you?" he replied. "Just to see what really happens when you're dead."

The coffin was lowered in and the two surly Bull Men were delegated to shovel back the earth and stones. George pulled his hat from his head with an uncouth parody of reverence.

All this time, the cassette player in the truck had been grinding out Dart's "hymn"; he switched it off now and addressed the congregation.

"My people, this is a solemn time, when a friend of ours, Hans Maastricht, finally loses his Shape. You all know he did wrong and did not obey the Master, which is me. So we bring him here to the Death Place to be taken up by the Big Master Underground and in the Sky, who watches over all of us, me included. His Whip is bigger than mine, and his wrath greater, and he's fast, so watch it. It takes a long while to acquire your Shape, but not very long to lose it. That's what it's all about.

"Okay, there goes Hans, who did not obey, who took to the bottle. . . .

"Now, my people, we will say the Creed, and I am watching to see that you all join in. Alpha, George, chuck in the earth . . ."

Whereupon he led the mourners in a chant, which, like what he chose to call his "hymn," was a cross between liturgical chant and acid rock.

> Four Limbs Long—
> Wrong Kind of Song.
>   No cause trouble.

> Four Limbs Short—
> Right Kind of Sport.
>   No cause trouble.

> Dare not to slay
> Do what they say
>   No cause trouble.

Speak only speech
Do what they teach
  No cause trouble.

The Master's is the Head that Blames
The Master's is the Voice that Names
The Master's is the Hand that Maims
The Master's is the Whip that Tames
The Master's is the Wrath that Flames.

And so on, much of it with gestures as to the parts of body referred to. The Beast People responded sullenly at first, looking out of the corner of their eyes to see who was or was not singing. But something like fervor sprang up among them, and they began calling louder and louder, and stamping, until lizards scuttled away among the undergrowth and pigeons fluttered out of the tops of the high palms.

A kind of mob psychology seized them. They started to dance, shouting more and more incoherently, and capering round the grave of their late friend. I saw Dart laughing, his face working as he kept up the chant. He cracked the whip in time to the beat.

Malformed legs and clumsy bodies pranced and quivered as a sort of conga line formed and shuffled round the clearing. Many of the rout clapped their hands above their heads like dervishes, chanting as they went. I stepped back to one side of the clearing to let them by.

While many abandoned themselves to grotesque joy, George's evil little eyes glanced about continuously. Others, too, as the singing rose to a roar, were keeping a furtive lookout. They might have been awaiting a signal.

Even as I realized who was missing from the crowd, I caught a glimpse of him, balanced on a strut of the pylon and half leaning on the trunk of a tree. Little of him was visible, concealed as he was, but I knew by the sandy head that it was Foxy. He had something in his hands. As I identified the barrel of a carbine, he fired.

He must have been holding the gun incorrectly. The impact of the butt—presumably in his chest—knocked him backward. His long ginger shanks disappeared into the undergrowth as I swung about to see the effect of his shot.

The singing died with the report. The bullet went chirping harmlessly among the trees. Everyone stood stock still.

"Kill! Kill!" George shouted. Waving his little thick arms

above his head, he charged toward the Master. After a moment's hesitation, the rest of the mob surged forward.

Dart paused only for a moment. The shot had nonplussed him; for once, he was at a disadvantage; for once, his nerve failed him. He started to run for the truck instead of standing his ground. And the Beast People charged toward him, crying for blood.

Dart reached the truck ahead of the pursuit and threw himself clumsily into the driver's seat. He started the engine as George flung himself against the door. At the same time, with great dexterity, one of the ape-men swung himself up over the back of the truck, and then on top of the cab. He was flung down into the back again as the truck jerked forward, but immediately reinstated himself.

The truck jerked forward a second time and then stopped. Dart was probably having trouble with his artificial limbs in the confines of the driving seat. The pause allowed several of the mob to throw themselves at the truck. They seemed to swarm over it. At that, I ran forward, shouting at them—otherwise, I was going to see Dart torn to bits.

Or so I believed. But Dart had his own way of coping with trouble. The muzzle of the riot gun came out of the cab window. I saw the flash as it fired. The mob fell back, and the truck was off, bumping toward the trail by which we had come. The ape-man crouched on the cab roof and made a jump on to the hood—but a low branch swept him off and he fell, rolling and tumbling in the dust.

George had been hit by Dart's shot. Blood streamed down his chest by his left armpit. He seized the wound, seized his face, plastered himself with dark blood, ran hooting and crying hither and thither among his companions, adding to their confusion. He was a terrifying sight. Everyone barked or yelled as they dashed about uncontrollably, trampling over the graves.

I had plunged after the truck, but the falling ape-man got in my way. Without waiting, Dart accelerated and was gone, bumping furiously down the rough track.

As I turned to hide, my Dog Man, Bernie, came running toward me. He looked as wild as the rest, so that I wondered if he were coming to attack; then the meaning of his frantic gestures penetrated. I swung about.

Foxy stood not a dozen paces from me, leveling the carbine at my head. There was no doubt where he had got the weapon from. Crouching, I picked up a shard of rock and flung it, just as the gun went off. For a second, I thought I had been hit. My head rang with noise. Foxy's shot had been decidedly more accurate than his first one, but had missed me. The shock threw me to the ground. Foxy also fell, shouting, so I must have hit him.

Bernie was at my side, yelling—I saw his mouth moving but could not hear. He grasped my arm as I heaved myself up and we ran into the undergrowth. I turned my head and saw some of the others, the Swine Woman among them, starting to head in my direction. That was enough. With Bernie guiding, we plunged through the thick bushes.

In those moments of panic, I believed that we were crashing through the undergrowth without plan. As I gathered my wits, however, I saw that Bernie was leading us along a path which wound upward and avoided the deepest thickets. I ran on behind him, in fear of my life.

The agony of keeping to Bernie's pace—we were running uphill—at least had the effect of clearing the noise in my ears. I forged on mindlessly, like a hunted animal. When he stopped suddenly, I bumped into him and clung to him.

"You good boy, good man," he said. He pointed forward with a misshapen hand and arm.

We had emerged on a cliff top. Below us a steep shoulder of rock, studded with bushes, rolled down to cliffs proper. Beyond lay the Pacific Ocean, blue, ever moving, yet seeming from this vantage point almost motionless.

Bernie patted me. "Good boy, no go back in water, you. Follow, follow, one at a time, take a little walk, hero—all be safe and no cause trouble, okay?"

"I can't climb down that cliff, Bernie, not to save my life."

He was already scrambling down the rock, clinging to grass and bushes. He looked up and smiled, his tongue half out of his mouth.

Craning forward, I watched him slide on to a ledge some feet below. He beckoned me. I stood where I was, afraid to follow. What decided me was a confused noise of pursuit in the undergrowth behind me. Clinging to the rock as best I could, I slithered down from handhold to handhold until I was leaning beside Bernie.

He began to move on at once and I followed. The path was now perfectly well defined, and safe enough if one did not look down at the extent of cliff almost below one's feet.

I saw there were round dry pellets where we walked, the droppings of rabbits or hares.

We continued for some way, encountering only two difficult stretches, where fissures in the rock had to be negotiated. When we reached a gnarled tree whose roots were embedded in the hillside, Bernie hauled himself onto it, we scrambled into the branches, and heaved ourselves up to more level ground.

He flung himself flat in the grass, then proceeded cautiously along, following the line of the drop. We crossed a small stream bed in which the merest trickle of water ran, and I recalled that I was parched with thirst. Through the trees growing all about us, ocean was still visible. Punctuating the sea below us, a large rock crowned with palms came in view. I recognized it as Seal Rock. Bernie and I had reached the highest point of Moreau Island.

Bernie slowed his pace and stretched out a warning hand.

We were confronted by a thorn barrier, threaded with barbed rattans.

I joined him and peered ahead through the screening foliage. Beyond the foliage was an open space with low meager buildings on its far side.

"Four Limbs Long Warren—he home there," Bernie said. "Warren, Warren, go see Warren, no shoot, okay?"

When I looked at him, he dropped his gaze.

"Okay," I said. "Go see Warren."

8

An Independent Point of View

Far, far overhead, pilotless B989s were crossing the sky; a faint rumble of their noise came to us. Otherwise, it was one of those perfect Pacific days that seem destined to continue for ever. The lusty young sun reigned in the sky, a slight breeze moved through the trees. Murmurous sounds of ocean filled the background. An occasional fulmar sailed across the treetops and alighted.

Over the buildings Bernie and I were approaching, complete silence lay. Nothing moved. I had kept careful watch as we skirted the thorn barrier, uncertain of our reception, but had seen nothing stir. Although Bernie pushed forward with confidence, my nerves were alert for fresh danger. I'd had enough shooting for one day.

The bungalows did not inspire confidence. All were the same size, all neglected; one of them, draped in creeper, looked derelict. Panes of glass were broken here and there. Aerials and solar heaters cluttered the roofs of the two more promising buildings. The complex was dominated by a three-tier lattice structure such as I had seen before elsewhere. It handled beamed power, as well as radio signals, while the global navigational system, linked to orbiting satellites, replaced an older system represented by the pylons rotting in the bushes nearby. This was where Mortimer Dart drew his power supply from.

I halted before an open door in what looked like the main bungalow.

"Anyone there?" I called.

Silence and the dull Pacific sound. I called again.

A lean man with white hair appeared round the corner of one of the buildings, an old-fashioned wrench in his hand. He stopped and looked us over from several meters away. He was naked to the waist and of a traditional shape.

"Hello, there, Bernie. Don't tell me that's something from Dart's laboratory you have there with you!"

"My name's Calvert Madle Roberts," I said. "I'm an American."

"Well, you're a long way from the stars and stripes here, friend." He came forward and said, without proffering his hand, "My name's Jed Warren. I don't have no nationality or profession."

I made no comment on that. He had a fine midwestern accent.

Bernie gave a long, confused account of how we had arrived. Jed Warren listened to it all without any indication of impatience or interest. At the end of the recital, he said, "You sure look like you been pushing your way through some mighty unfriendly territory. Guess you both better come in and wash up, since you're here. I just hope you don't bring no trouble with you." He cast his gaze meditatively round the clearing, but all was still.

I followed him into the building. Bernie would come no further than the step. I was able to strip off my overalls and lave my arms and face, which had suffered a thousand scratches, under a cold shower in Warren's washroom. I stood there with my head up and my mouth open, letting water pour into my parched mouth. After a few minutes of that, I felt decidedly more human. Going outside again, I was pleased to see that Warren had brought Bernie a bowl of water, in which the Dog-Man soaked himself.

Warren wore an old pair of trousers and plimsolls. His torso was tanned a deep brown. He was so thin that every rib showed like a bar. A straggle of white hair on his chest matched his untidy beard. The hair on his head was long, drawn back, and tied with a strip of fabric behind his neck. He was about sixty years old.

"I take it this ain't in the nature of a social visit," he said.

"No. As Bernie said, we were lucky to get away with our lives. Foxy managed to get Hans' carbine up from the lagoon."

"He's a troublemaker, is Foxy. Different altogether from Bernie. And George got shot?"

"A flesh wound only, I'd guess. But George is in a difficult position now that his friend Hans is dead."

"Since I ain't a sociable man, I'm right glad to hear this ain't a sociable visit, Mr. Roberts. I suppose that you'll be heading straight back for Dart's place, now that you're refreshed."

"Can I radio the ASASC in San Diego from here?"

"You can't do nothing from here, excepting leave. Facilities are kind of limited, as I guess you observed."

"Mr. Warren, you don't make a man feel very welcome."

"I didn't shoot you, did I? I'm busy with something, if you must know, and I want to get on with it. Now why don't you and Bernie head right on back down that trail and see how Mortimer Dart's getting along."

"Are you anxious about Dart? I got the impression you two weren't on very good terms."

"We keep clear of each other, that's the main thing." He stood there unmoving, waiting for us to leave.

"We go, good boy, yes, no cause trouble," Bernie said, casting anxious glances at me.

"I've not come here just to be turned away, Mr. Warren. I want refuge. You may like to know that a Search-Rescue party is looking for me even if I don't get a call through to them. They'll be here within forty-eight hours, at maximum. I shall then make a full report to the appropriate authorities of what I've seen on this island."

He spat on the ground. "Appropriate authorities. . . . Why, if that ain't one of the phrases I came here to escape from. It makes my hackles stand up, that's what it does. Appropriate authorities, my left foot. . . ."

"As you may imagine, Mr. Warren, every one of the Beast People will be a living witness to the unholy goings-on here. As you can further imagine, the island will be cleared. You'd better further imagine what could happen to you if you were implicated in the proceedings."

Warren put his arms akimbo, still hefting the wrench, and looked me in the eye. "You turn very threatening all of a sudden, Mac, when a man don't lay on a red carpet for you. That's the way folk are, I guess, and that's why I don't make you welcome. But just you tell me—who do you think these appropriate authorities are as is going to be surprised at what they come across on Moreau Island?"

"You're American, Warren, aren't you? From the Midwest. Well then, it's the American government that will be surprised at what they find here. Not to mention the Army, and the Co-Allies. When the media get on to what's happening here, they'll blazon it—and your part in it, whatever that part is—all round the civilized globe."

He swung round unexpectedly and caught Bernie a smart blow on his haunches. "Beat it, Bernie! Go home to Master!"

Bernie gave a yelp of pain and started running. When he was some distance away, he turned and looked back. I called to him. But Warren made a stone-throwing motion with his hand, and the Dog Man disappeared into the bush.

Warren turned back to me. "Now we'll talk, Mac."

"My name's Roberts, not Mac, Mr. Warren."

"Now that creature is out of the way, we'll talk over what you just said to me. First off, we'll take a speedy look around my pitch. Maybe you'll learn something, maybe you won't."

I would not let my anger show. Instead, I walked with him, believing that I might well see and learn more than he intended me to do.

It was a brief walk. He did no more than take me round the outside of the buildings. He had a sort of glorified junk-yard out back, stacked with old oildrums and crates with U.S. naval markings, and piles of metal scrap. Warren evidently fancied himself an artist, for the rear of one bungalow had been painted with a crude fresco, while other large paintings, executed on board, stood about in the sun. There were also abstract figures built from the metal scrap, elaborate and tall. One of these, unfinished, stood by the back door. More distant was a pool with glass over it; I caught the glint of a fish in the water. We walked past the leading foot of the power lattice and returned to the front of the building.

"So you see, Mr. Roberts, there's quite a lot of junk around supplied direct by the U.S. Forces. One of their nuclear submarines calls here with fresh supplies every other month. Who do you think built this here power unit? Dart and me with our bare hands?" He laughed. "Where do you think Dart gets all his finance from for his research? It ain't from me, I'll tell you that. It comes out of the long pocket of the American government, that's where it comes!"

The mind indulges in strange tricks. As soon as Warren began to tell me—no, just before he began to tell me—my mind released the truth to my consciousness. I had known for some while. It was impossible to believe that this island would remain unvisited and unsupervised. Yet I had managed to believe it because it was better than believing that Dart's unhallowed experiments had the backing of any nation, particularly a Co-Allied nation like the United States.

"Why should they support Dart?" I could hardly speak.

Warren laughed. "You can't have seen into his laboratories down there, or you wouldn't ask such a question. I ain't going to tell you. But I'll tell you this much—if you're aiming to let out word of what goes on on this island to the media, then you're the one who's going to be in trouble when the sub calls again. Oh boy, will you be in trouble! One word and you'll be behind bars for the duration. You'd better see the error of your ways, friend, and pretty soon, because that old sub'll be calling in a few days."

I cleared my throat and looked at the scenery for a moment or two, while he stood and looked at me.

"Mr. Warren, I must tell you that I'm desperately appalled by what you tell me. You're claiming that all that goes on on this island is okayed—subsidized—by some government department?"

"That's what I'm saying." He put the wrench down on the step to study me more comfortably. "There's a war on, as you know. What goes on here has been taken over as vital wartime research."

"Mr. Warren, you seem a decent enough man—do you think the war is sufficient excuse for the cruelty and misery inflicted on the creatures here? Aren't we supposed to be fighting against just such hellish injury to life and spirit? Are you out of your mind up here?"

To do myself justice, I must say how empty my words sounded even to myself, even in that time of shock. As a trusted servant of my country, I was in a position to know how many projects were subsidized by the taxpayer and had to be kept secret from him, because of their dreadful nature. On a smaller scale, the same thing applied in my own government department; endless confidential projects were afoot, and I knew them only by code name, if at all. In war or peace, it makes no difference. I was one of the few people who knew of the dreadful weapons being stockpiled on the

Moon, some of them destined for use in the Pacific theater. Yet one evil never canceled out another.

He dropped his gaze, saying nothing.

"Come on, Mr. Warren, tell me how you like being a part of this organized torture! You may reckon that I'm in a tricky position. Don't you think your own position is a whole lot nastier?"

He straightened up angrily, sticking out his bony chest.

"See here, I'm not a part of anything, so don't get any wrong ideas. You don't know my history, any more than I know yours. We're strangers, and strangers have no right to pry—"

"Speak to the point. What are you doing here? If what you say is true, then you're part of the payroll of Moreau Island, aren't you?"

"Look, mister, I never had no affection for society in any way. I was born in a big city, and, just so soon as I could read the signs, I lit out of there for the country as fast as I could get. I was a dropout, like so many others back then. A hippie, I was. Only most of my buddies got married or got a job or something and dropped back in again. Me, I stayed out. But they got me when the war came and conscription come in. I was so blamed antisocial in the Navy that they gave me a posting to work for Dart. I quarreled with him the very first week I was set down on the island, and I've lived solitary up here ever since. So you can't say I'm a part of anything that happens down below in his place. Am I now?"

"You maintain his power supply, you remain on the payroll. You're implicated all the way."

He wiped his hand on his mouth. "You shouldn't say those things to me. I hate what goes on, same as you do. Only I seen lives being crushed out of shape everywhere, as long as I been around to see. . . . You better come inside. I need a drink. Maybe you could use one, too."

"Thanks. I could. Any fruit juice would be fine."

"You'll have to have what I got, Mr. Roberts."

We went in. Everything went on in one cramped but neat room; Warren lived, slept, ate, and cooked there. He brought two beers from an old fridge. We pried open the cans, raised them to each other, and drank. I did not tell him how long it was since I had swallowed beer. It tasted wonderful.

"I agree that many aspects of human life have always been wretched. Sometimes it seems that the most promising

advances of science merely leave us with more problems—
just as the lowering of the infant mortality rate landed us
with world overpopulation—but you have thrown your lot
in with an experiment which promised nothing but misery
from the outset. How can you possibly defend that?"

"Don't I keep telling you? I ain't defending anything. I
opted out. Besides, what can one guy on his own possibly
do?"

"I don't imagine anyone ever heard Jesus say that."

"Well, so happens I ain't Jesus, mister, so let's leave him
out of it! I do the best I can, and that's enough. I'm keeping
out of the war, I ain't killing no one. If you want my opinion,
the world's gone mad."

"You could sabotage Dart's power supply."

"He'd come up here with the Beasts and kill me, and the
power would be working again within a week. Drink up, and
you better be on your way. I'm sorry I ain't more hospitable,
but you make me feel bad."

"It's not me, it's your conscience."

"No, it ain't. It's you and remarks like that one you just
uttered. When I'm on my own, I'm perfectly dandy."

Again, silence fell between us. I felt his resentment. My
hand holding the beer can trembled. My thoughts were wild
and troubled. So contaminated was I that it seemed as if I
had lived all my life on Moreau Island, my initiative—despite my efforts—perpetually taken from me, as if I were no
more than one of the Beast People. And I said to myself that
when I returned to so-called civilization I would have to
resign my government post and live privately. Of course,
there was still the question of returning . . .

"Mr. Warren, you say a supply submarine calls here every
two months. Tell me more about that."

"I told you. It calls regular, leaves stores and anything
special Dart has ordered. Brings mail. It's due again in four
or five days."

"Dart drove off, leaving me to fend for myself. He cannot
be sure whether I am dead or alive. Is it possible for you to
radio from here?"

"I got no radio, not even a receiver. All that kind of tackle
is down the hill."

"Then I want you to let me stay here until the sub comes.
I will not get in your way. I won't even talk, if you want it
that way. Just let me wait in safety for the sub. Dart will

think the Beast People killed me and will not come searching for me."

"Nobody on that sub's likely to agree with your line of talk. They'll tell you there's a war on, same as I tell you."

"Mr. Warren, you aren't on anyone's side, are you? You aren't on Dart's side, and you certainly aren't on mine."

He wiped his lips on the back of his hand before replying.

"Goddammit, Mr. Roberts, I'm on my own side. Dart'll never rest till he finds what happened to you. All I want is a peaceful life, and a man has to strive hard to get that. You're just the latest in a long, long line of people been interfering with me and trying to make me change my tack. I ain't having any, so that's final."

"Are you afraid of what might happen to you?"

"There you go, another of them snide remarks! No, I ain't afraid. I'm just my own man, that's all. I believe in nature and beautiful things, which somehow don't include my fellow men. Besides—let me tell you, there's reason to be afraid here, if you happen to be disposed that way. You come on out the back before you get on your way, and I'll show you something to make your hair curl!"

This was a surprising break in his increasingly surly mood. I followed him out past the unfinished sculpture, and beyond the power lattice. He picked up a metal strut on the way, looking about as he did so, and saying that he never knew when he was being watched.

"The Beast People would not attack you unless provoked," I said.

He made no answer.

The track narrowed, rising slightly, and we walked through a stand of bamboo, the leaves of which moved continually in a slight breeze. Then we were through them. Confronting us was a stupendous view.

Warren had led me to the extreme eastern tip of Moreau Island. We stood on a shoulder of rock from which we could survey uninterruptedly the eternal ocean, the compass of the horizon, and the great dome of sky overhead. The little topknot of Seal Island was also visible, almost at our feet. The antique noise of ocean pounding on rock dulled in our ears.

Because the afternoon was far advanced, the sun was moving toward the western sky. It flooded the empty world with its radiance, and lit the sails of a ship far out to sea. My heart leaped at the sight: the vessel resembled an old sailing ship—yet that was mainly because the naked ocean allowed little hint of scale. The ship I watched was almost a mile long, its hull sectioned plastic, its sails metal foil. Those sails and their rig were controlled by computers, and the computers were checked out occasionally by a crew of two trade unionists.

I had sailed on one of those beautiful cargo vessels, years ago. My third wife's family owned a shipping line; the voyage had formed part of our honeymoon. That marriage had long been dissolved and was a thing of the past, like many of my personal friendships.

I became aware of a tension in Warren, and turned to find him staring fixedly at me.

He wet his lips. "You ain't feeling any compulsion to jump, by any chance?" he asked.

"To remember, but not to jump."

He shrugged and looked away from me.

"Only a month back, one of Dart's experimental creatures escaped and headed up here same as you done," Warren said. "Dart and Hans and George and some of the others come up in pursuit with guns and nets. I hid out in the bushes."

"What happened to the creature?"

"Why it ran right to this very spot and then it stopped— 'cause it couldn't get no further, could it? It was a cross between an ape and a man. The others closed in on it and— you know what it done? Rather than be captured, it threw itself right off the rock and down into the ocean. If you go out on to this promontory of rock, you'll see the cliff's so steep that a man might dive clear from here and end up safe in the ocean, given a bit of luck. Take a look for yourself."

I worked my way along the narrow promontory, feeling that mixed dread and fascination for heights of which even space travel had never managed to cure me. The rock outcropped. As Warren said, it would be possible to take a leap and fall clear of the cliff into deep water. But that fall was all of a hundred meters; I would not have liked to try it.

"What happened to the creature that jumped?"

"Drowned. Hadn't got no arms to speak of."

I turned, and he was coming at me with the strut raised, mouth set in a line.

He moved at the crouch, ready to strike. When our eyes met, he paused momentarily.

"Warren—" I said. My back was to the precipice.

He jumped at me.

The pause had lost him his best chance of getting rid of

me. I had instinctively taken my balance, and I was heavier than he was.

He brought the metal bar down hard, but I took the blow on the left shoulder and, with my right hand, reached out and grasped him round the neck. He tried to kick my left leg away. I grappled him nearer to me until he dropped the bar and began to punch me in the stomach. I'd worked my right hand round his skull, and got my fingertips into the socket of his right eye. He yelled. He got a lucky kick under my kneecap. My leg buckled and I went down, taking Warren with me.

We lay across the rock, my head hanging over into space. Warren had sprawled on top of me but I got both hands on his throat, and my right leg round one of his.

"Lay off, you bastard, before we both go over the edge!"

I gave his neck a twist for luck, and then pushed him from me. He sat gasping in the grass, alternately feeling his eye and rubbing his throat. As I stood up, I saw that the metal strut lay behind me, lodged precariously where it had fallen, in one of the ridges of the rock. Picking it up, I flung it far out to sea, turning away while it was still twisting in the air toward the water.

"Get up!" I said.

"Don't throw me over, mister! I didn't mean you no harm, honest. I must have been crazed in the head. . . ." He crouched at my feet, one arm half raised in a protective gesture.

The realization came on me that I was trembling in every limb.

"Get up," I said. "I'm not going to harm you."

He climbed slowly to his feet, watching me all the while. We glared at each other like a pair of hostile cats. I observed that the trembling had hold of him too. His face was deadly pale. We went back to his place without speaking.

At the bungalow, with one hand on the lintel of the door, he paused and looked into my face, his mouth working.

"You really aren't intending to finish me off, on account of what I did to you?"

"All I want is to remain here. I told you. I'll leave you alone, you leave me alone. I shall wait here until the submarine comes, and then I'll get aboard it."

He dropped his gaze.

"There's a total war on, Mr. Roberts. Nobody aboard that sub's likely to listen to one word you may say. I respect you as a merciful man, but you're as mad as the rest of 'em."

9

Revels
by Night

That night was calm. The breeze died; an almost full moon shone down on Moreau Island. I slept on a bunk in one of Warren's outbuildings and was tormented by evil dreams.

I was walking through a thicket of bamboo, in a confusion of light and shade. Suddenly, I came upon George, the Boar-Hyena Man. For a moment, I could hardly make him out; then I saw how blood ran down his face from a wound in his head, where the skin had been entirely torn away, leaving an ugly gash amid his thick curly hair. The streams of blood surrounded his deep-set eyes, running in the furrows of his nose and about his mouth. As he breathed, bubbles rose and broke in his nostrils.

Even as this terrible sight transfixed me, George jumped from his place of concealment and threw himself upon me. I awoke groaning, and was unable to calm myself until I dragged myself from the wretched bed and walked round the room.

After that, I unbarred the door and stepped cautiously outside. It was too hot in my bungalow—the air conditioning had broken down long ago. I leaned against the brickwork and breathed deep.

To my left, the ocean glinted through trees. Its slumberous

roar came clearly through the night air. Overhead, more than one AES moved; some of them contained nuclear weapons, which could be guided to any desired target below. The island—isolated though its sordid dream might appear—was a part of the mainland of world tragedy.

A nightbird called. Otherwise, the island was hushed. The world also paused. This early stage of the war was widely recognized as a preliminary pause to gather corporate strength and will, during which appearances suggested peace; while, behind the scenes, enemy governments maneuvered for strategic positions, allies, total mobilization, and diplomatic formulas that would exonerate them from blame when the storm broke. As yet, only local actions had been undertaken; few had died; only tactical nuclear weapons had been used. But no one doubted that devastation on a hitherto unimagined scale was on its way. As yet, the birds still sang. But a final time clock had already started ticking.

While I stood, breathing deeply of the night air, the door of Warren's bungalow opened. I happened to catch sight of the movement by the widening of an angle of shadow, although the hinges were entirely silent. The gleam of a gun barrel showed before Warren himself stepped forth.

"Oh, it's you, is it?" he said. "What'n the hell you think you're doing strolling around at this time of night? I thought as we had visitors."

"I wanted some air. Go back inside."

"You set a mighty chancy business going here, Mr. Roberts. Like I told you, they're going to come looking for you, and then I'm going to be in trouble."

"The better I get to know you, Mr. Warren, the worse I think of you. On your own admission, you are in your present predicament because of your loathing of your fellow men. You can hardly expect them to have mercy on you."

He digested that. "Then you must be a bigger fool 'n me, because you never heaved me over the cliff when you could have."

"I have religious beliefs, which occasionally prevent me from committing murder."

"That accounts for your habit of saying things to make me look small. What are you, a Mormon or a Catholic or something? They used to make a lot of trouble where I lived." He leaned his rifle against the wall, as if he felt inclined to talk. Why not? I thought, since we were all doomed anyway.

"My parents were Protestant, though we rarely went to

church. We used to sing carols at Christmas. Last century
and this, the Christian God has become discredited because
he is identified more and more with materialist progress. So
I don't think I pray to him.''

"Something in what you say. My folks was religion-mad,
and much good it did them. You got some fancy religion of
your own, then?''

"I've no patience with all the fakes who have been
dragged in from the East to take God's place, your gurus and
maharishis and swamis and the rest—the incense-and-flow-
ers brigade. Nor do I see anything but placebos in the new
science-based religions, like scientology or ufolatry. I'm
happy not to believe in Dart's Big Master in the Sky either.''

"That don't leave you much.'' He chuckled.

"Right. This hasn't been the best-ever century for faith,
and some would say hurrah for that. No, I believe in a sort
of abstract God, remote and not particularly comforting,
whose specialty is continuity rather than succor. The universe is his—I mean, it makes more sense to think of a
consciousness behind creation than to imagine that it all
grew in its complexity out of nothing, like a mushroom out
of concrete. But now that the universe is a going concern,
my God is aloof from it—maybe he is now powerless to
interfere. You could say he was more of an Artist than an
Administrator.''

Warren grunted. "He sounds a worse dropout than me.
You'd be better off worshipping a little brass Buddha than a
God like that!''

"I agree. Except I don't believe in brass Buddhas. Oh
God, I disbelieve—help thou my disbelief! The only contact
my God has with men is that he is manifest in trace elements
in our best aspirations. When you aspire to do good in any
field, then you are furthest from yourself, and so nearest to
God. It's up to you to keep the contact. It's not up to him.''

Warren listened to what I had to say with close attention.
Poor fool, to be taken in by what I said, I thought; of course,
he would be a sentimentalist at heart. I realized as I was
talking that my belief in God was hollow, I no longer believed in anything.

Only a year or two ago, as the ideological blocs moved
toward conflict, I had argued that God was the greatest invention of the human imagination, and merely a positive goal
toward which we were all moving, generation by generation.
The idea was that we should gradually evolve into a kind of

godhead. Even as I expounded this view, I was moved by
my own faith and sincerity; besides, it suited eminent Un-
dersecretaries of State to speak of profound matters. People
had listened.

Most of those people were now in uniform or subterranean
bunkers.

After a knotty silence, Warren said, "It ain't for me to
stake my claim that you're talking nonsense. For one thing,
I know that you're better educated than me, just to hear the
way you make with the words. But I guess my view is that
mankind has somewhere, somehow gone wrong, and ended
up too complicated. I'd agree with the Bible where it says
that big cities is sinful—that I do agree with. No doubt but
the Bible has a lot of sensible things to say, like 'An eye for
an eye, a tooth for a tooth.' But the only time I get a glimpse
of any durn God is when I look around me at the beauties of
Nature."

He indicated the silent scene around us, still bathed in
moonlight, and its stately tranquility.

I had been aware of light scuffles in the undergrowth while
we were talking. Now the vague indication made by Warren's hand directed my attention to a clump of bushes, dark
and indeterminate, which grew under a cluster of palm trees.
Had I seen something move?

Warren, too, appeared to have seen or heard something.
He stretched out a cautioning hand to me, peering ahead,
before reaching to grasp his rifle.

Tropical places generally have their share of nocturnal
birds which forage in the undergrowth. Their rustling can
conjure up all kinds of nervous fears if one has reason to
suspect danger. We stood there, together yet separately,
listening to the discreet noises. They seemed to come from
all sides of us.

He turned back to me, saying in a low voice, "Is someone
there, do you reckon?"

"Dart doesn't travel easily. He'd come in daylight."

"May not be Dart . . ."

A cloud began to cross the moon. Immediately, a heavy
crashing came from the thickets on our right, as if someone
or something had decided to take advantage of the temporary dark.

"They're there, right enough," Warren said. "They've
come for you. This is your doing, confound it all, coming up
here talking about God and getting me killed."

"We'd better get inside. They may go away by daylight."

He did not heed me. Instead, he ran into the middle of the clearing, raised his gun, and fired two shots. The noise was transfixing. Long after the actual shots had died, the echoes of them went racketing out across the wastes of the Pacific. As the echoes were still hurtling toward infinity, nearer sounds spoke of a big creature crashing away through the bushes in panic.

Warren stood where he was, gun half raised.

"Whoever it was, he's gone," I called.

"He wasn't alone by any manner of means," Warren replied grimly.

Almost as soon as he spoke, an answering shot came from the jungle. I recognized the report as that of a carbine. Foxy? Next moment, ill-defined figures rushed into the open from several directions, converging on Warren. I called to him. He raised his rifle and shot one of the charging figures stone dead before the others overwhelmed him.

I saw an oil painting in the backwoods of Austria once which represented the ultimate in self-betrayal. Two murderers in hunting outfits beckoned a young man into a gloomy forest. It was evident, even from the sickly smile of the youth, that he would never emerge living from that remote spot. But the two murderers had so cozened him that he was about to go with them voluntarily, unable to face the fact of his imminent death, thus deceiving himself as much as they deceived him.

As I ran back into my bungalow, I felt it as an act of self-betrayal. It would have been nobler to have thrown myself into the middle of the clearing and died attempting to rescue Warren. But an instinct of self-preservation hurried me inside and slammed the door behind me.

From the window, I was able to get a view of what happened to Warren. His attackers numbered at least ten. Among them, I thought I recognized the active Alpha and Beta, the two ape-men, and the grotesque form of the gray Horse-Hippo. Standing to one side, apart from the fray, was Foxy. He held himself like a man; the resemblance was heightened by the confidence with which he now carried his carbine.

By some miracle, Warren broke free of the pack and ran for the undergrowth. Then he swerved, as if suddenly becoming aware of what he was doing, and doubled back toward the buildings. I saw him running toward me.

One of the monstrously heavy Beast People—a creature that had been lurking undecided out of my line of view—bore into sight, charging at the running figure. Warren saw it, raised his arms, swerved slightly, and came on.

The charging creature had its head thrust forward. It cannoned into Warren just as he reached the next building. It made no attempt to pause or even to seize Warren, plowing on like an express train and crushing the man against the wall. Warren uttered one gasping cry of agony and collapsed. The brute, stunned, fell beside him. Immediately, other creatures ran up, throwing themselves on Warren in frenzy.

They began to tear his body apart, to rip his clothes and his limbs away from his body. Only Foxy stood aloof from the scrimmage. He came closer to watch the destruction of the body.

So ghastly were these scenes, enacted in the bright moonlight, that I remained where I was by the window. The realization that their sport would soon be over and that they would then be after me—presumably their original quarry—threw me into a sort of dazed resignation without being able to shift me from the horror of the scene. Only when some small torn thing struck the window and slid down it, three inches from my face, did I pull myself away and think of escape.

The building contained equipment for the solar plant overhead. Against one wall was a metal staircase leading up to the roof, and so to the great lattices outside. Since there was no place to hide inside the room, my way lay upward.

Fortifying the outer door with old packing cases, I climbed the stair. It was difficult to see, and for a while I sweated and struggled under the roof, trying to pull back the bolts of a trapdoor. They gave at last. I pushed open the door and had a refreshing prospect of roofs, dark trees, moon, stars, and the lattices of power above me. I saw that night was sick and dawn near; bars of cloud drew across the eastern sky, the pallor of day radiated from behind them. The sun would soon come thundering out of the Pacific. It was an encouraging sign. Foxes prefer to hunt by night.

There was no way of locking the door behind me. I closed it and looked cautiously about. I was on a small platform. Solar heaters stood on the roof nearby. A ladder led up from the platform into the girders above. I was safe here only until

I was noticed. All I could do was crouch, hoping that the Beast People would go away.

They showed no sign of doing that. Their bloody party with Warren was almost over. While some of the smaller creatures still scrabbled with his torso, the others, as I could hear, were barging about round the buildings. The voice of Foxy came to me: "Search out other Four Limbs Long, heroes!" I hoped that fear of human habitation would keep them out of the bungalows and eventually drive them back to the bush. Alternatively, I hoped that they might all break into Warren's bungalow, so that I could make good my escape then—the oncoming dawn should provide me with enough light to see my way downhill to Dart's fortress.

Now they were investigating the buildings. I could hear their thick grunts and voices. I crouched where I was, scarcely daring to breathe, the fate of Warren ever present in my mind.

They began to hammer on doors—whether mine or Warren's I could not tell, since the roof obscured my view. Glass shattered. That was a woof of pain. Idiot scampering feet. Yelps and exclamations, thick quarrelsome voices. More sudden smashing—clearly from inside—yells, snatches of mad song. Another crash, insane laughter. "The Shape you're given the day you're born/Is lost when we put you under earth." Furious shouting, a blow, whimpering.

Then I saw one of the hideous Swine Women trotting across the broken ground, holding a can in one hand and her ripped trousers in the other. She was being pursued by a hairy creature resembling a bear. As she ran, she made a shrill noise—impossible to say if it was from fear or mirth. The bear caught her and, as they fell together, her can went flying. Liquor spilled from it.

They had broken into Warren's place without fear, and were at his beer supply. The knowledge gave me fresh heart. As they became drunk, they would fight among each other and forget me.

Relaxing slightly, I stood up to ease my limbs, turning to catch the dawn breeze as I did so. I found myself staring into a pair of eyes only a meter or so from me.

The nearest leg of the power grid rose beside the bungalow. Clinging to its diagonal spars was one of the ape-men, Alpha or Beta. There was no mistaking that misshapen head, with its baby skull and nose like a tapir's. It clung to the mast with both hands and held a beer can by the rim in its mouth.

Neither of us moved. I had no weapon. A fresh outbreak of screaming came from below. I let out a yell, flinging out my arms. The ape-man opened his mouth, letting the can drop but catching it economically with one hand. He did not fall as I had hoped. He let out a paralyzing answering yell, swarmed through the lattice of the mast, and hurled himself at me.

There was a thin guardrail round the platform. It formed a slight obstacle between him and me. As he landed and clung to it, I thrust my right arm out and caught him a tremendous jolt under the chin with the heel of my open palm. Then I kicked the paw that clutched the guardrail.

He fell back on to the roof, roaring. On the margins of my vision, I glimpsed the Swine Woman and bear creature stand up, point at me, and scream with rage. It was time to escape. In any case, I did not fancy myself in a fight with Alpha or Beta, whichever he was, and he was already picking himself up.

Throwing open the door in the roof, I saw in the pale wash of light below that my room was already invaded. One of the Beast People walked there alone, beer can to mouth, his free hand making airy circles above his head as he staggered silently round the room. I slammed the door. Nothing for it but to jump from the roof.

I went to the edge and peered down. The madmen were about, laughing and running, but this was no time to make any sort of a choice. The ape-man was coming up behind me. I jumped, staggered, and fell to the ground.

As I pulled myself up, the ape-man landed beside me, taking the fall better than I. He wasted time bellowing his discovery, so that I started to run even as the others responded and came up. I went to double round the buildings, away from the sea. My way was blocked.

A vile creature with bloody visage stood there, swaying slightly and waving some sort of weapon in his right hand. He had been eating from it. The unsteady light was sufficient to illumine one of Jed Warren's forearms.

Others were there, figures out of a hitherto undiscovered representation of the nether world. My heart quailed within me. The ape-man seized me from behind, grasping my shoulder.

I turned to evade his other hand. The Rhino Man who had

crushed Warren came bursting up behind and barged him out of the way in crazed eagerness to get at me. It was my chance. I dashed between them and ran for the nearest bushes.

I was in the open. On the extreme margins of my vision —I dared not look to left or right for fear of falling—a gaunt figure rose and aimed a gun at me with a hunter's deliberation. I dived into the bush as the carbine went off. The bullet plunged away harmlessly.

Pulling myself up, I saw that the pursuit was now on. Ill organized as they were, some of them drunk on Warren's beer, they could nevertheless hunt me down and destroy me. I was human quarry, by my very shape marked out as one of the enemy. They would tear me apart until that hated shape was no more. They would rend my flesh and eat my tenderest parts.

As I ran through the bush, I could think of only one hope —to catch Foxy unawares and take the carbine from him. With the leader disarmed, the rest of the mob would come to heel. My best hope was to climb a tree and wait. But there were no trees here that could possibly be climbed. They were either lofty palms or small thorns and bamboos. To hide in the bush was impossible—these creatures would unhesitatingly smell me out.

Some dreadful being, heavy and insensate, was plunging along in the bush to my left. I stopped for a moment, and he stopped too. Was he pacing me, simply for the pleasure of the hunt?

Sudden hope filled me. "Bernie?" No reply.

"George?" No reply. I began to run again, and the hidden thing began to run too. For him, this was a game, and I was game. As in a trance, I plunged through the colorless jungle of dawn, not heeding how I scratched or tore myself in my flight.

Like a clear, clean vision came the thought of that high eastern cliff and the jutting rock from which Warren had tried to push me the day before.

I would jump!

Even if I never survived that terrible fall, at least I would be free of a far worse death. There was no other escape for me, as the shouts and yelps all about me made clear. The pack was closing in.

I bounded through the bush in what I believed to be the direction of the cliff. The creature on my left kept pace with me. Occasionally, I saw its monstrous form through the swinging foliage.

Noises sounded ahead—shouting and crashing. Again I swerved, and in a moment arrived at a clearer patch of ground. The ocean glinted ahead. With one sweep of vision, I took in a far glimpse of sun—a chip of it merely, only the merest segment of it cutting above the horizon and sending a dazzle across the ocean in the very instant of its rising. Dark cloud piled above it, but that first ray lit me—and lit two of the Beast People plunging up from my right flank.

Only a few meters lay between me and the rock on which I had fought Warren. I knew my one hope of making that leap was to plunge forward without pause or hesitation, or my courage might fail me. I had stepped from spaceships into the gulfs of space, but this was a challenge of a different order.

What finally spurred me was the bestial face of a Swine Man who came bursting out from my left. He it was who had paced me, who now moved in with smiling yellow teeth for the kill. Swine he was, but I read vulpine ancestry there as well in the sweep of his fangs and cut of jaw under that piggish snout. He stretched out his arms, and I ran like madness itself for the high cliff.

The Swine Man screamed with fury. Seabirds burst from underfoot. The universe wheeled about my head. I saw the cliff, the supine sea, the jut of rock, saw my death on the rocks beneath, ran even faster.

My courage had fled. But it was too late. I bounded along the jutting rock as if it were a diving board above a pool, shouted with all my strength, jumped. The Swine Man tried to stop too late, toppled, fell with a great cry. Lucifer without grace.

As I plummeted, all fear left me. I fell with arms and legs outstretched, performing slow cartwheels in the air. I saw the place I had left, the cliff wall, the expanse of sky, the sea, the creature who fell some distance from me. I fell, and a muddle of thoughts coursed through my brain. I even recalled the old idea that one relives one's past in such moments before death; yet I could recollect nothing but the terrors of my days adrift at sea and the secrets of Moreau's researches—even in this extremity, I was not free of the island.

By bracing my body and getting control of my limbs, I was

able to stop tumbling and plunge down feet first. The drop seemed to last for ever—yet equally the ocean came rushing up to meet me at incredible speed. As I closed with it, I saw that I was free of the rocks. The tumbling creature who kept me company at some distance did not look so lucky.

Just as I hit the waves, the sun appeared to sink back below the horizon. It was as if I had traveled back in time—on the level of the ocean, sunrise was still an instant away. The water was dark. It struck me hard and swallowed me.

Everything became confused. I had not fallen straight. The breath was battered out of me. Beneath the water, dark shapes of rock loomed, or so I thought. I tried to find my way to the surface, became lost, saw red and green streamers of light explode about me, lost consciousness.

Not entirely. One rarely loses all awareness. But my senses became detached, and I could do nothing effective. Except drown.

Yet I did not drown. The muddle and pain that saturated my being finally receded like a tide. I was aware of people about me, of a thatched roof overhead. Hands were on my naked body. A remote but sensuous pleasure had roused me. I closed my eyes in extreme languor, only opening them again with an effort.

I lay in a rough hut. Two Seal Men knelt to one side, smiling and nodding when they saw my eyelids flutter. Over me, her lank hair trailing against my skin, was a Seal Woman. She performed a kind of kiss of life upon me, although her lips were not fixed on my lips. I gave a great cry as realization dawned on me, and all my limbs trembled in a bout of rapture. Then I sank back into a deeper oblivion.

10

After
the Fall

Of my four-day stay on Seal Rock, I prefer to say as little as possible. Some acts which seem beautiful and natural and profound at the time of their doing are distasteful in memory. And one person's pleasure can arouse disgust in another. Perhaps this is particularly so among Western nations, where sexuality is even today regarded more ambivalently than in the East.

Emotions that move us most deeply often undergo metamorphosis after the event.

The name of the Seal Woman was Lorta. There were four Seal Men of roughly her age over whom she had complete sway. They doted upon Lorta, and it was easy to see why; she gave herself to them with an inexhaustible abandon, with such joy that even I, at the time, felt no shame in accepting her loving. She ruled them completely because they ruled her; she could not resist them because she was irresistible. And such was her bounty that those Seal Men felt no jealousy of each other, or even of me, a stranger. Theirs was a good fortune, and they had the wit to know it.

The names of the Seal Men were Saito, Harioshi, Halo, and Yuri. Between our games of love, we swam and played in the ocean. And we conversed—conversation for them was also a game. My comprehension of what they were saying grew fast, and perhaps they spoke more comprehensibly from having to talk to me. I learned that the Swine Man who had fallen from the cliff top with me had plunged to his death on the rocks. Crabs and sharks had devoured him. Since crab formed a considerable part of the seals' diet, this was particularly good news to my friends.

I learned also that it was the Seal Men who had dived in the lagoon and retrieved Maastricht's carbine. They had given it to Foxy in exchange for a gift of berries and stolen canned syrup.

They knew of the submarine. But their time sense was deficient, so that they had no idea of when it might visit Moreau Island again, or of how long it was since it last called. In many respects they were like children, and their charming child-faces puckered with laughter as they confessed their ignorance.

No, I betray them by expressing it so. When I was with them, it was otherwise—I am back to my old stiff self again. Of course, they knew about the regular visits of the submarine. It was a treat to them, the arrival of that fabulous unfeeling monster out of the ocean depths where they could not go. They used to follow it into the lagoon and sport beside it, making obscene gestures and playing intimately with each other—which made them very popular with the crew.

They did not know when the vessel had last arrived, or when it would come again. Why should they? It had no significance for them. They laughed heartily at the idea that I should wish to climb into and be shut away in the submarine, and would not accept that I was serious when I spoke. As for confessing their ignorance—they were not burdened with our guilts about knowledge or the lack of it.

I say they were like children. What I mean is that they had never accepted the rules that most of us accept. They remained astonished by the world, and by their luck in being part of it.

Although they did not have an arm or a well-formed leg or a proper hand between them, the force of their characters, Lorta's in particular, insured that they survived in a bubble of happiness. The warm ocean helped; it was their amniotic fluid, and held no harm.

They had a religion of sorts. Maybe it was a deep and complex religion, and I was not with them long enough to understand it. Prig that I was, I tried at first to explain my religion, as I had with Warren, but I might as well have tried to persuade them to live on dry land. They had a belief in a shark-shaped Spirit of the Deep (perhaps it looked rather like a nuclear submarine), which inspired a pleasurable terror in them.

I must come out with the truth. There was also Satsu.

When Seal People escaped from Dart's laboratories, they lived along the more hospitable northern coasts of the island, until Dart instigated a hunt and shot one of them, a young woman. Then they took refuge on Seal Rock. Other children were born to them but did not survive; Satsu survived and flourished. She was a normal little Japanese girl, full of vivacity, with all limbs intact.

Satsu was four or five years old—so I estimate, for nobody knew or cared. "Year" was a word without meaning to them; they thought in terms of tide rather than time. She was treated like a little goddess, a queen, a naughty sister, a pet monkey. She sang and played and ran, she could climb trees faster than an ape, she swam better than her parents, she joined with glee in the love games of the adults. She was as pretty as paint.

There it is. For some, I detail a picture of depravity. At first, I was shocked by Satsu's love activities, particularly when she was the center of the group's attentions. I did not even know that such young children could experience orgasm. But so it was. Their naturalness was such that I quickly became used to everything that went on; my initial resolve to devote my energies to restoring Satsu to a normal environment faded to nothing.

Also, I became the delighted and responsive recipient of this dear child's attentions. Laughingly, her mother and her men encouraged Satsu to join in our raptures. I developed ideas of my own, and took the initiative. The sun and the sea were all part of our involvement.

"Calvary" they called me. So I remained on that happy rock, being fed and making love in a variety of ways which I had never dared to imagine before. In that timeless period, I lazily watched as the sun rose and traveled its great course through the sky. When it sank toward the west, an immense shadow grew from Moreau Island and swung out across the waters to reach us, but it never quite got that far. When it was within a few meters of our minute shores, the sun would break free of the last westerly rocks of the island, dramatically reappearing, and the long chill shadow fell away on its own coasts, so that sunset was golden and unbroken for us.

In the language I began to learn, the sun which dominated our every day was referred to as "Lob-Chy." I did not know whether this was a Japanese word adopted from the language of my friends' ancestors, or a corruption of the English word "love child." I hoped it was the latter.

We generally swam near the rock. I swam with them. Although I never entirely cured myself of a dread of the abyss beneath us, I felt secure in their company.

In the complete nudity of my new friends, in their complete lack of reserve, I greatly rejoiced. I was so far seduced as to wonder whether I could not remain for ever on that patch of land; I daydreamed about a time when the rest of the globe destroyed itself, and I swam forth with my friends and lovers to populate the planet with a new sort of human being, whose aggressions were sublimated in total voluptuousness.

Unhappily, I remained part of the warring world, and it remained a part of me, in a way that was alien to them. I had to go back. I had to deal with Dart and the problem of the submarine. I had to return to the island, and to affairs in Washington.

And it was time for me to leave. There could have been no sybaritic life for the Seal People with me there; I upset the delicate balance of their existence, for I was a large extra mouth to feed, and I could not hunt as they could.

Before I went, it occurred to me that there was one gift I could give them. They ate their fish, crustacea, and seaweeds raw; and I knew that there were occasions after rainstorms when they huddled together cold and miserable. I could teach them how to make fire; with fire they could warm themselves and cook food.

Among their few possessions were numerous old Coca-Cola bottles and cans in which they stored the rainwater they collected. Taking one of the bottles to a flat slab of rock on the north of their sanctuary, I broke it and used the base as a crude lens. Focusing on scraps of driftwood and dry kelp cast up in the last storm, I patiently nursed a few sparks into existence. How Satsu chirped with delight as the smoke came up! Blowing carefully, I conjured a flame. Soon we had a small fire going. I speared a fish on a twig and cooked it on the flame, before giving half to Lorta and half to Satsu. "Clever Calvary!" they said.

They spat it out and made disgusted faces, but I explained that they would soon become used to the taste and prefer it to raw fish. They thanked me cordially. At least the novelty of the fire delighted them.

It was after midday when I set out to swim to the island, which acted as planetary body to the little satellite of Seal Rock. All my friends came with me, including little Satsu, swimming on either side of me. At the mouth of the lagoon, I heaved myself ashore and sat there, hidden from anyone who might be prowling the island, while I waved the others goodbye. They promised to see me again, departing with fond and lascivious gestures.

Putting on the shirt and trousers which I had carried in a bundle during the swim, I turned and made my way cautiously ashore.

Moreau Island looked as I had last seen it.

No work was being done on the quay. The lagoon lay silent and undisturbed. The crane remained in the shallows where it had fallen. A seabird perching on its exposed superstructure rose up and flew slowly away to sea as I approached. Otherwise, I observed no movement. The village of the Beast People lay apparently deserted on the other side of the water.

My reasoning was that Dart would be pleased to see me after the recent troubles; I could pretend to fall in with his wishes, and await the arrival of the submarine. When he went to meet it, I would follow and overpower him, and persuade the submarine commander to carry me back to the States. The commander could easily radio his base and verify my identity. I could then report the situation on Moreau Island to a higher authority and see that those who wished it were restored to civilization.

I walked toward the palisade surrounding Dart's HQ, alert and watching for possible trouble.

Someone was standing motionless under the trees, just a couple of meters outside the gate. I paused and observed him. It looked like George, the Boar-Hyena Man, but I could not see for the boughs of trees.

Making a wide detour, I approached so that I could have a better view of the figure, making my way eventually along the outside of the fence.

It was George. I could hear the flies buzzing about him.

A tall stake had been driven into the ground. George had been impaled upon it so that he stood up almost as if he were still alive. His face was far more dreadful than it had been in my dream. He looked to be staring fixedly across the lagoon, through the cloud of bluebottles which sipped at his flesh.

Sickened, I backed away. This crucifixion was more cunning and sadistic than anything the casual brutality of the Beasts could devise. Yet who else would have done it? I could only suppose that Foxy had inspired it. The mystery remained how Dart could have allowed them to do it so close to his fortress.

There had been a change in the balance of power here in the short while I had been away. The very silence of the place emphasized that. It was significant that it was George who had paid the price. His position as Hans' foreman had put him on untenable middle ground. His enmity with Foxy (so I assumed) had sealed his fate. But how many others had died?

Aware of the possibility of a trap, I retraced my steps along the barricade without calling to anyone inside.

As the terrain grew more broken, my way became more difficult, but I worked toward the back of the enclosure where the laboratories were. Here I stopped. I could hear something moving about on the other side of the palisade.

Why I did not call out, I do not know to this day. It may have been because there was some quality in the movements which made me uneasy—something furtive and at the same time irascible. I stood where I was with a dry mouth, listening as the unknown thing passed unseen within a meter of me.

Standing there as if accursed, I saw a long pole lying nearby. It had a diameter of some fifteen centimeters, and had probably been used for scaffolding when building was in progress—or so I guessed. When the sounds on the other side of the barricade had died away, I went over to the pole and tried to lift it.

It would not move. Only when I levered it from side to side did it budge slightly. It was wedged between loose rock. I kept working, and eventually managed to pull it out. It was three meters long.

With a great deal of effort, I pulled it back to the front of the barricade, as near to George as I cared to get. He was unnaturally still—that was what was frightening about him.

Then I let the pole fall forward so that the top of it protruded over the fence. It gave me a ramp up which I could climb.

The falling pole started an alarm buzzing somewhere inside the HQ. I heard it buzz on and on without answer. Making as certain as I could that I was not observed, I ran up the pole and dropped over the other side. I flattened myself on the ground of the enclosure and listened. Only the buzzing of the alarm, on unendingly.

As I rose to my feet, Heather came to the window and beckoned to me. My relief at seeing her was great. I had almost begun to believe that everyone on the island was dead.

Heather made frantic gestures and disappeared. Never had she looked so animated. In a moment, she was unlocking the house door and letting me in.

Her dark shoulder-length hair looked somewhat disheveled, but she seemed much as she had the last time I saw her. She was wearing her tunic outfit and sandals. Catching my glance, she gave me a quick seductive smile, moving her whole body as she did so.

"Calvin, you can't know how glad I am to have you back!" She clung to me. Automatically, I put an arm about her, thinking how strange it was to hear ordinary English spoken, to have myself misnamed, to be within four walls, to feel the bite of air conditioning, to hear—yes, a symphony of Joseph Haydn's was playing quietly throughout the building. Everything was so *dry*. A picture rose before me of Lorta's damp, agile, insatiable little body; it denied all that herein was, just as all that herein was denied her body— despite the girl who now clung to me. The moment gave me an insight into Heather; she too was a sensualist, but her sensuality had been devoured by what we call civilization. Her intellect and her instinct were at war—she could never be comfortable. I would meet nobody like Lorta again. Nor would I ever attempt to describe her to anyone; she would sound like a whore, a nymphomaniac—whereas the truth was that she was free, uncalculating, the very reverse of this cultured pussy.

"Where is Dart?" I asked, disengaging my arm.

Heather stared at me curiously. She put a finger to her mouth, in a gesture I recalled.

"We thought you were dead for sure, yet here you are, looking really pretty chipper. . . . One more death and I'd go out of my mind. It's great to see you. . . . Aren't you glad to see me at all?''

Automatically I said, "Yes, I'm glad to see you." I was too, if only remotely; this was a girl I could not handle.

She grunted. "You're a formal bastard, aren't you! Typical politician. Don't you ever relax and be yourself?"

I laughed. "What mixed-up questions you ask! Where's Dart?"

"He's ill." Pouting at me.

"What's the matter with him?"

"You'd better come and see him, if you have such a preference for his company."

Without further word, she led me to the corridor I knew, past my cell, through a red door, and along an infinitely richer corridor, with abstract paintings hanging on the walls. The carpet underfoot was worn by parallel tiremarks. At the end of the corridor, Heather motioned me to wait and went into a room whose door stood open. There was a muttered conversation, and then she motioned me into Dart's presence.

Dart lay on a bed in a room that was a combination of bedroom and surgery. It had no windows. Comsat pictures flitted across one wall. Mortimer Dart was propped up by pillows; he nursed a riot gun by his side. He would be unable to use the gun; his wheelchair with its cyborg arms stood grotesquely to one side of the bed; a robe covered the puny little extrusions on his shoulders.

He wore a bandage round his head like a turban. It covered his left eye and part of one cheek. I saw deep scratches running down his cheek, neck, and chest. His right eye stared at me with an unspeakable wrath in it.

Somewhat shaken, I went to his side and asked what had happened.

His voice was thick, scarcely recognizable.

"I shall be all right in a day or two. I'm well doped. It's fever—I caught it by that bloody grave. You must guard this place until I get better, now you're back. They attack at night. They'll be here again tonight. How did you get into this building?"

I told him, and his hot gaze went to Heather.

"You were supposed to be keeping a watch. They'll kill us if they get in here. They've tasted blood and a bit of power. It's no joke. . . . A phrase keeps going through my head as I lie here. One of old Nietzsche's, I shouldn't be surprised. Power corrupts, but a bit of power corrupts absolutely. That's what's got into *them*. I should have put them down long ago, Bella and all. You and Heather and Da Silva must take it in turns . . ."

"What happened to you?" I asked again.

"I told you. I got a fever at the Death Place. And the ride shook me up. I relaxed my guard—you can't trust anyone, Roberts. When I think how the world set itself up against me even in my mother's womb, I don't know how I've survived so long. One day when I'm better, I'll pull this whole bloody island down into the sea. . . ." He relapsed into a fit of choking.

I looked inquiringly at Heather. She gave me an eye signal and said to Dart, "We'll go and pull that pole away from the fence now, Master, so that we'll be safe. And I'll be back to see you soon. Just lie quiet."

Out in the corridor, she was clutching me again.

"It's fever, Calvert. He's rambling. I've got him doped, but I'm so scared, really. This is a hell of a position to get in."

"What happened? Did Bella attack him? Where is she?"

"I don't know for sure what happened. It was Bella okay —hey, you don't imagine I scratch like that, I hope! My guess is that he fell or tripped or something, and she attacked when he was down. I didn't dare go in. He fired at her and she disappeared."

"She's with the Beast People?"

"Oh, how I wish she were! No, she's somewhere right here. She ran through to the laboratories and locked herself in. Cal, you'll have to go in there and kill her—and anything else you find in there alive."

I liked the way they all assumed I was on their side.

We unlocked the outer door and went into the compound, where Maastricht's paint cans still lay around. I could smell George over the palisade.

"Let me out and I'll drag the pole in here. Then nobody else can use it." I had accepted the idea of siege without question.

"Can't you get rid of that grisly object they stuck up out there?"

"Maybe at some other time."

"That stink would make me throw up, if throwing up wasn't so undignified . . ."

Considering the circumstances, Heather was cool and efficient. I tried to feel less hostile toward her as I heaved the pole into the enclosure. She stood by the gate and kept watch. I recalled that she was a karate adept and knew that she would be prepared to use her art on the Beast People if the occasion demanded.

In short time, we had the pole stowed against the stockade and the outer door locked again.

As we went inside, glad to be away from the sick-sweet aromas of corruption, I said, "Dart left me to die at the cemetery—I've been through hell to get back here. You wouldn't fetch a guy a sandwich, would you?"

She said, "I guess I'm worrying too much about Morty. He'll lose the sight of that left eye, unless he strikes lucky. . . . Sure, I'll fix you something to eat—you must be hungry. Then maybe you could use a shower and change of clothes. You smell almost as high as George out yonder."

Yes, a civilized girl, I thought. I'd been away for four nights, and four nights' survival on Moreau Island was like a century elsewhere; all she said was, "I'll fix you something to eat." She was wise not to wish to know what had happened to me.

I wasted no time thinking about her. As soon as I heard her in the kitchen, I was through into the other corridor, trying each door as I came to it. With the second door, I was in luck. It was the radio room. I went in, locking the door behind me.

The amount of equipment was imposing. Most of it was familiar. In fact, most of it was a standard USCF station, an Mk IV MVFQ12. It hummed contentedly to itself, its tapes alert to roll when triggered by any incoming signal. Beautiful was what it looked.

Tuning in to the San Diego wavelength, I switched to Send and put out a carrier. Response almost at once. Crisp American voices came up, and a few seconds later I was speaking to Captain Jimmy Hobarts of Naval Search-Rescue. As precisely as I could, I gave him my geographical position and outlined the situation.

"Sounds like home from home," he said. "Hang on." Silence for ten seconds. "We'll have a Navy chopper over from Fiji base for you. Should be with you—wait while I get a weather check . . ."

I could hear the background noises of his office in San Diego before he came up again. "Weather in your area is set fine for the next twenty-four hours, though enemy interceptor activity is reported. But we'll order the chopper to keep low, and she should be with you in, say, seven hours, seven and a half. No, later. Eight hours maximum.''

I looked up at the clock. The time was 1609. It would be midnight before the helicopter made it.

"I'll be waiting," I told Hobarts.

"They'll have room for five people and a stretcher case, okay?''

"More than enough." I gave him a number to dial in Washington, to alert my department of my continued existence, and he acknowledged.

"See you."

Let's hope you will, I thought, as I switched off. Midnight was still a long way off.

11

Another Visitor for the Big Master

I was in command of my own destiny again, as far as that is possible in our complex societies. The war was making changes in everything. Old orders and states might be going down in murk, and new ones rising; but at least radio stations were still manned and helicopters flown. Those were the kinds of things I understood and set store by, although my experience on Seal Island was still too vivid for me to rejoice in them at present.

No matter. Arrangements could be made. Administration could take over from chaos. I was thinking ahead even before I left the radio desk. When the helicopter arrived, Dart, Heather, and Satsu would go aboard with me. Dart needed hospitalization.

I would make a report on conditions on the island directly I returned to Washington. An official inquiry would follow, and a shakeup for whatever department funded the experiments so laxly. Those experiments would be investigated, closed down, and financial support withdrawn, if I had any say in the matter. A skeleton medical administration would be established to see that the Beast People were humanely treated for the rest of their natural existence. It might be as well to suggest sterilization, in order that they should not breed a further generation of unfortunates.

Right. With Dart out of action, that left only two problems to be sorted out before midnight. Those problems centered round Bella and Foxy. Bella had to be found and assured that no further harm would come to her. As for Foxy, I thought that if I could only reason with him, then he might bring the Beast People under control—perhaps we might make him their legitimate leader—then we might expect no further disruptions of law and order.

There should be no more bloodshed. While talking to Foxy, I also wanted to find out what had happened to poor Bernie. It might be possible to take him to a happier life, if he still survived. I might even be able to find him a light menial job at home, maybe on my father's farm.

So much I determined to my satisfaction before leaving the radio room.

Heather was outside the door.

All softness had left her. In the lines of her face, the tensions of her body, I saw a lethal determination. She was covering me with a weapon I had seen before—the twin of the one Da Silva had toted a few days earlier. I saw that my moment had come. Truth sprang up, fanged, between us.

Neither of us needed speech. She had caught me in the radio room and was intending to kill me! I was going to stop her, and disarm or kill her.

I jumped at her.

But it was a long jump; in the electric air between us, I saw her right arm come up. Without otherwise changing her stance, she fired the weapon at me. It made a noise like *ZZlitt*, very quietly.

It works on compressed air, I told myself irrelevantly, while my knees collapsed and I fell forward, trying but unable to clutch at a burning sting which radiated from under my left shoulder to the rest of my body. Heather stood back and watched me go.

All my muscles had gone slack. There was no way I could save myself. I fell like a doomed tree, rolling over to lie face upward in a crumpled position. Heather stepped over me, looking down with a professional coldness more ghastly than hate.

Heat coursed through my body; I thought I was dying. Yet my brain remained lucid. Detachedly, I decided that I had been hit by a needle containing deadly poison which worked instantly.

Meanwhile, I heard Dart calling feebly down the corridor. Heather stooped over me and said, "The Master always thought you were an enemy agent. I did not, but it seems that I was wrong. Now I can check." She went into the radio room. I had heard what she said, but it was difficult to put the words together and make sense of them.

I lay there while whole landscapes of pain and time came by. Eventually, Heather reappeared. She stepped round me and disappeared in the direction of—what was that man's name?—of Dart's room.

More landscapes, more eternities. I tried to think of Lorta.

Heather was back, and bending over me. She lifted my head.

"Cal, I know you can hear me. Listen, you are in the clear. Every message leaving here is automatically recorded, so I've been able to play your message back. You're in the clear. You're no enemy agent, you're just the goddamned blundering shipwrecked politician you always claimed to be. I'm going to give you something to counteract the anesthetic that's gotten into your system, and you'll be right as rain again in no time."

The fighting woman was set aside. With nurse-like care, she propped me up against the wall, fetched a hypodermic, and injected a clear fluid into my bloodstream. Then she brought me a cup of coffee—real and not synthetic coffee. Time began for me again.

She got me to my feet and half dragged me to my old bed, where she made me comfortable.

"You tricked me, Cal, you bastard, asking for a sandwich," she said. "I was a fool to be so easily fooled. It's worked out okay—you're in the clear now. The Master was convinced that you were not what you pretended to be. I suppose you know why?"

I didn't know why, but I was unable to speak, to put my question into words. I could feel the antidote working, stirring me up.

"Now I've got to adjust to you as someone with a lot of pull in Washington," she said. "It's funny having Mort in bed in one room here and you in bed in another. . . . It gives me the chance to intercede for him. He really needs more funds and more assistants; the Department is so stingy in that respect. You could put in a good word for us. I know you're prejudiced against what's going on here, Cal, but I'll escort you round the labs, which you haven't visited yet, and you'll see how well run they are, despite our difficulties. We need your help, Cal, really . . ."

She sat on the bed and snuggled against me, looking down sweetly into my eyes.

"It was the Department sent me here. I have trained with animals. The Department's idea was that I should be Morty's personal bodyguard and assistant . . ."

Her warmth and her pleasant perfume were things I fought against even in my weakness. I also rejected what she said, and croaked in protest.

"You didn't know that, Cal, did you?" She gazed rather wistfully into space. "Maybe Morty's twigged by now. Remember when Islam was on the warpath and at the same time Cuban forces invaded Samoa? A bad time at home. I arrived on Moreau Island in a private plane, courtesy of the Department, letting on I was escaping from Samoa. Morty accepted me and my story. And why not? He knows the whole damned world's falling apart. . . ." She sighed.

Silence lay heavy in the room—the roaring I heard was not of the ocean outside the building but of my inner ear, where tides of life were returning. Then she spoke again, her lips close to mine.

"What I want to put across to you, Cal, is how important Morty is to the war effort. I'm proud to serve, to *do* something, anything—to feel that at last I, well, it's hard to put into words, but I guess at last I have a job here which is equal to my capacities. Sure, I get bored at times, because of the isolation, but it isn't every woman who finds the kind of opportunities I do here. I mean, I'm doing a man's job—well, more than that . . ."

She squirmed and settled lower. "Give it eight or maybe ten years, and I think we'll see a woman President of the United States—what's left of the States, anyway. My boss in the Department feels the way I do."

She stroked my face.

"That is one plus you can mark up to the war. I know it's awful, thousands of people getting slaughtered like cattle all over the globe, but at least attitudes are clear-cut and you can see them as they really are. No pretenses. People are either your friends or your enemies, you know what I mean? I mean, either *we* win or *they* win, and that simplifies all sorts of issues. It's like watching an old gangster film, in a way."

She was lying against me now.

"You *must* give us a good report when you get back to Washington, Cal. Otherwise, it could be *you* in trouble. I mean, it is wartime, and secrets have to be kept. You threatened the Master with death and he didn't like that. . . . We're your friends, remember. Okay, you don't exactly go for some of the things that happen here, but far far worse things go on in the Soviet and Islam blocs, on a far far larger scale. Moreau Island is just a drop in the ocean. People have to suffer . . ."

I managed a loud groan.

"Cal, are you getting any feeling?"

"What department employs you, Heather?" At last I got the words out.

She smiled. "That was what had the Master puzzled, I guess. You see, we're funded here by *your* department—the Department of State. We assumed that if you were who you claimed to be, you'd have known all about Moreau Island all along."

Life and control were returned to me. Perhaps the shock Heather had given me helped. I persuaded her to go and get me some food and drink and sat on the side of the bed. It was 1710.

Her revelation would make no difference in terms of what I had to do when I returned to Washington. I would make my report and tender my resignation. Somewhere in the building in which I worked, maybe in a safe in an office in my corridor, was a file. It would have a fancy code name. In that file lived Moreau's other island, a doppelgänger of the real island, a tidy little utopia docketed into paragraphs and subheads. It would make dry legal sense. It would be an abstract. And there would be neatly entered figures, with all columns carefully balanced by accountants once a year.

It was that other island I had to destroy. The real island could not exist in its present form without that other shadow island in a file in a safe in my department in Washington.

Carefully, I levered myself off the bed and began pacing up and down. When Heather returned with a neat little snack on a tray, I was feeling more the man I used to be.

As I finished the meal, we heard a distant crash.

"That's Morty," Heather said, looking alarmed. "He's trying to get out of bed. I must go and look after him, or he'll do himself an injury."

I sat alone for a moment, then rose, left the room, and walked quietly along the main corridor. Heather had gone down the side corridor to Dart's room. I continued until I came to the door opposite the control room. It served as one of the entrances into the laboratory area.

Although Heather had offered me a conducted tour of the labs, it might be a better idea to have a look on my own. For one thing, I wanted to find out what had happened to Bella. Heather had claimed that Bella was at large in the labs; but the more of Heather's statements that could be checked against reality the better.

I listened outside the door. I tried the handle. It was locked, as expected. In the control room were monitor screens, some of which would show me what was happening in the labs, of that I felt convinced. Before trying them, I called Bella's name softly at the lab door.

At once, there was movement in the room beyond. Someone had been standing in silence listening to me. There was a sound like a snake crossing a bare plank floor. A key clicked in the lock. As the door began to open, I knew it would not be Bella standing there.

What I did see was a thing so fearful, so unlikely, that it might have stepped from the pages of an evil fairy story. I stepped back a pace as it spoke.

"I do not know who you are," it said, "but if you are in the Master's service then I must welcome you in."

That perfect diction, even and well turned! How much more acceptable were the shattered vocabularies of the Beast People, reflecting in every distorted syllable their distorted lives.

The creature confronting me was even more of an aberration of the human form than they. It stood under one and a half meters high and was disproportionately thick of body. It had extremely short legs, so that the arms trailed almost to the ground. Its head was distorted into cephalic form, the skull tapering almost to a point at the rear. This cranial abnormality was emphasized by the creature's lack of hair.

Distorted bone structure also accounted for the ugliness of the creature's face, which was inordinately fleshy. Its forehead bulged and came low over the eyes, while the chin curved upward almost concealing the mouth. There was no nose to speak of. I was reminded of drawings of the faces of seven-month fetuses. Yet the overall effect of the creature was of a malignant gnome.

Natural disgust at being confronted by this figure was increased by the curious quality of its skin, which had a dead, grayish color and the texture almost of scales, so flaky was it. The gnome was encased in sloughed snakeskin.

Because it was forced to gaze up at me, the impression I got was of a long-drowned face. Even the eyes looked watery and without life.

Yet it moved naturally and easily, standing aside for me to enter the room and even extending a hand to me. The nails of the hand curved protectively right over the tips. I could not take hold of it.

"Bella," I said. "I came to see Bella."

"Did you, indeed? Bella caused a great deal of destruction, I fear, so we had to take care of her. She is dying in the next room. We persuaded her that her life was not worth living, and gave her the wherewithal for suicide. You have no need to worry further."

"I must see her. Take me to her quickly."

As I started forward toward the door the gnome had indicated, he said, "You Father People have many impulses." So uninflected was his diction that I could not tell whether he spoke in envy or sneeringly.

The room I was in was the first of the laboratory complex, which was full of different rooms and divisions. This anteroom was an office, an array of filing cabinets and a computer terminal being the chief things I noted. What caught the eye was blood everywhere, as if a battle had taken place. In the corner by the far door lay four small gnome bodies, dreadfully mauled.

The next room, a full-blown laboratory with expensive equipment grouped about it and rows of cultures under glass along one side, presented a scene of even greater havoc. I marveled at how many of the gnome-men must be housed here. At least a dozen of them lay sprawled in death about the room. I saw by their wounds that Bella had killed them. They lay in their own blood, the heavy smell of which saturated the air.

Bella herself lay in one of the far corners. Her wig had fallen off and I thought she was dead. Four of the gnomes stood alertly by her, arms hanging by their sides. Two of them were women, by their dress. Like the men, they lacked hair on their heads. As they turned to inspect me, I observed a slight development of breast tissue beneath their blouses.

They started to ask my name, but I ignored them and went to Bella. As I knelt by her, her head came up angrily off the floor. I jerked back so that she would not bite me. But she recognized me and said, "You Four Limbs Long, you no like see me get whip." She closed her long eyes.

A broken plastic hypodermic lay by her side. There was blood all over her tunic and her malformed hands.

"Why didn't you go to your own people when you had the chance to escape, Bella?"

"Own people make me death, same I go along Master too long time." She started to pant. "Bella smell like Master, make trouble."

I took her head in my arms, and she let me do it. She was no more than a dying animal, yet—such was the will to communicate between us—at this moment she was perhaps more human than she had ever been. Words and thoughts still struggled up in her beast brain.

"I do good best thing here—try make death Master, make death many bad small peoples here. All kill, best thing. No more trouble, finish get whip."

"Yes, yes, Bella. This place is evil. Soon it will be closed down."

She seemed to misunderstand. "Bella all close down, dear thing." She choked on that odd endearment, then lifted her head for a moment. "Bella go get more trouble from Big Master in Sky now."

What passion tore me?

"It's not like that, Bella! That's all a lie. There's no Big Master in the Sky. After death there's nothing, nothing at all. Silence, Bella—just silence. Just peace. No Big Master." No phantom files where you're an entry in a budget account. Just damn all. That's the best thing to believe, Bella. No other islands for you to go to.

"I believe you will find that the animal is defunct," one of the gnome women told me. When she touched my shoulder, I moved it away.

Lowering Bella's head to the floor, I got to my feet and marched past the small people. They were making some sort of ponderous technical comment on the situation, which I did not heed.

Why was I seized by such grief? It cut me like a knife. It was as if I had thrown away my own life. The contemptuous face of my first wife came to mind—I had hit her and she had turned away in disdain, with no word. . . . I hurried from that place and went back to my bedroom, where I stood for a while with my head in my arms and my elbows resting against a wall. Bella's warm animal smell still clung.

I could have wept for the sullied animal innocence of Bella. Instead, I reflected with shamed intensity on the evils that had attended my stay on this nightmare slab of rock.

Before my eyes rose an electromagnetic spectrum of earthly torment, in which all that could happen to a man was ranged in order, from Best Event at the light end to Worst Event at the dark. On such a spectrum, there was no place for concepts like Good and Evil—I thought of the clichés I had uttered on that subject, and could have laughed. The lightest color of the spectrum was a completely fulfilled and giving sensuality, the darkest was represented by the nameless things with which I had just come in contact.

How deluded I had been, and how secure in my delusions! And I was to blame for much that had happened. While Dart was responsible for his rule, I was also guilty. In a flash of terror, I saw myself back in Washington, turning up the Moreau file, issuing my blanket condemnations—only to find my own rubber-stamp signature on the original authorization. . . .

My arrival on the island had been the signal for a chain of death.

Hans Maastricht. He had managed to drink and work safely enough for years before I came and upset his balance. And from his death, all the others had followed. I had refused to retrieve Hans' gun from the lagoon. So Foxy had got it, and had injured and eventually killed George. That disruption of Hans' burial had driven me to seek out Warren, with the aid of Bernie. Of all victims, Warren was the one for which I most blamed myself. In that ghastly night during which he died, I believed that the faithful Bernie might also have been killed—and if so, he would have been killed because he had befriended me. . . . Then there was Bella. . . .

But there my self-recrimination ran its course. Why, I'd be beating myself over the head about my past wives next. It was useless to wallow in guilt. The way of redeeming myself was to act now, to try to fulfill the rest of my plan regarding Foxy before the helicopter came. I saw clearly that I also had to have a firsthand account of the creatures in the lab. Dart should give me that, now.

I looked at my watch. It was 1751. Plenty of time. It wasn't even sunset yet.

12
The Frankenstein Process

The Master was propped up in bed, his head and half his face still swathed in bandages.

"Perhaps you can recall to your mind, Mr. Roberts, an earlier little chat we had concerning who was fighting this war. I believe I put it to you then that it was caused by you normals and not us freaks. The affair's grown so big that we're all involved. You don't realize how deeply I am involved—this isn't a fun-fair I'm running here, you know.

"Since we have finally established that you're the stuffed shirt you always claimed to be—one more pompous politician whose left hand doesn't know what his right is doing— let me tell you that top military and medical men have been flown out here from Co-Allied war teams many a time, to kowtow to me and pick up a smattering of new gen from me, if they were lucky. Right, Heather?"

She was standing by his bed, looking remotely at a spot on the far wall. She nodded.

"You see, you think you're in the swim, Mr. Roberts, but you don't know what the war's all about."

"When you have finished with the generalities," I said, "you'll recall that I asked you for some rationale, however sketchy, of those gnome creatures who killed Bella."

"Those gnome creatures, as you call them, go down in the books as SRSR, right? They're the SRSRs, Roberts, and not gnomes, whatever your demented mind may despise them - as. Perhaps you'd like me to tell you what that appellation stands for. SRSR stands for Standby Replacement Subrace. Standby Replacement Subrace. And that's exactly what they are. Mark I.

"I intimated to you earlier on that I am running a complex program here. The SRSRs are the culmination of one stage of it—it's as simple as that. They're what this island's all about. McMoreau's crude vivisection techniques were just an amateur beginning. After that came my early experiments in genetic surgery, of which, with regrets, only the two ape-men, Alpha and Beta, currently survive. They represent a deep line of research, toward the goal which I was always aiming for.

"You see what a prenatal drug did to me—used randomly with random effect. Since thalidomide, a whole new range of drugs have been developed to govern cellular and glandular activity. The difficulty was to test them out on human stock under controlled conditions. There's a limit to what you can achieve with any number of guinea pigs—mice, rats, monkeys, frogs, and all the rest. You need human stock, it's as simple as that.

"That's where the Beast People came in handy. Next best thing to humans. I was able to make the progress here, safe on my little island, denied to countries with all sorts of pettifogging antivivisection laws.

"It's me, and me alone, who has developed these SRSRs, despite a few toffee-nosed biologists and whatnot who drop in from time to time." His lips trembled, as if he was overcome by the thought of them. "I've no clue what you think of me, Mr. Roberts, and I don't much care, but let me tell you that I—me, without hands or feet—have achieved more than Columbus or Genghis Khan. It's no good me explaining what I've done because you wouldn't understand the terms involved, but, basically, I have developed drugs of two kinds which operate radically on the fetal structure.

"One drug (collectivum) alters the fundamental epidermal functioning to give a protective outer covering much like a snake's scales which inhibits certain types of radioactivity. The other drug inhibits the stimuli of cellular activity, and alters various basic metabolic rates, especially the entire pleiotypic program.

"Using these two drugs in varying combinations on fetuses provided by the Beast People, we have developed—I cut a long story short—the SRSRs, a true subrace, who have several advantages over the human race."

"Advantages?" I asked.

"They are immune to certain radiations lethal to us, gestate in only seven months, mature early, bulk less, consume less food, less oxygen. All telling plus factors in the sort of catastrophe scenario they are designed for."

Incongruously, while he was talking scenes of rural peace slipped across his wall, accompanying the slow movement of a Haydn symphony. Old whitewashed houses with wooden tiles, slow women with buckets at long-armed wells, decrepit fencing, tremendous meadows fading into mist, old men in old hats, stooks of corn, mountains, streams, oxen dragging decorated carts, reindeer, lime and acacia trees heavy with flower, children running down a lane—these images welled up and died in time to the music.

I said heavily to Dart, "What sort of satisfaction do you feel now that your work is finished?"

"The work's far from finished, make no mistake. We have the SRSRs—and three of the best specimens are now in the States being studied—but they are not yet perfect. They have to be made to breed true, to reproduce their own kind and not monsters. At first they were infertile, but we've licked that one. Now one of the females is with child, and we have high hopes about that. But much has still to be done. Rome wasn't destroyed in a day, as they say."

"Why are you doing this? Why should governments involved in total war countenance such inhuman experiments?" I asked him. "Of what use are your SRSRs—how do they increase our happiness?"

"You're not so smart as I took you for. I thought you would have grasped that, pal. Right, you mention total war —what's the outcome going to be? The Co-Allies will win in the end, but they're going to win at a hell of a cost in lives lost. You think I don't care about such things, but I do. A world of want is going to result—that's the cost of victory, and that's where it's at. The human race will be decimated, air and ground will be radioactive."

He sat up more positively in bed and clasped his thin chest.

"But if we can breed up the SRSRs, they can take over the enormous tasks of reconstruction. They are already receiving indoctrination in Co-Allied aims. They will be less vulnerable to radiation than the rest of us, will propagate faster, will consume less supplies because of their smaller bulk. They are, in fact, our survival kit into the future; they may even replace us. And even if the picture isn't as gloomy as I have painted it, then we'll find other uses for them. Waste not, want not. The SRSRs would be ideal as crews for spaceships. You may yet see them go out and explore the stars while poor old mankind stays at home—what's left of it. . . ."

If this monster was to be believed, then I was witnessing the culmination of the Frankenstein process. The first tentative steps that Victor Frankenstein had taken, as recorded by Mary Shelley, toward making one life that stood outside the natural order of creation, had led to this; that a time could be visualized in the near future when the natural order would be entirely supplanted by the unnatural. The arguments of logic, with appeals to progress and the necessity of survival, were employed by Mortimer Dart much as they had been by Frankenstein and, for that matter, by Mc-Moreau.

In this spectacle of perverted propagation, I was lost. There was no possible dialogue I could have with a man like Dart.

"Things have got out of hand," Dart said to Heather, groaning. She laid a hand against his cheek in a sympathetic gesture. They exchanged eye signals which I could not interpret. I stood where I was, thinking fast. I was horrified by what I had seen and learned, and I would act as soon as I was in Washington. Dart's experiments might be valuable to the war effort, or they might not. But they were certainly grossly mismanaged; none of the killings need have happened in a properly run organization. Dart was no better at ordering his affairs than Wells' Moreau had been.

Reflecting on the rundown state of the island and, in particular, on the lack of staff—why was there no American nursing personnel on duty with the SRSRs?—I understood, from long experience of similar projects, that Operation Moreau was being wound down. The fact might not yet have dawned on Dart, but his grand schemes had already received a thumbs down back home. He had been superseded. Maybe the old cloning programs of the eighties had been dusted off and given new life; his researches had already been written off or superseded. However that might be, I suddenly knew in my bones that Dart was through as far as funding went.

And wouldn't he be mad when he found out!

It was likely that he would kill the SRSRs. And me too, if I was still around. He might be pathetic; he was also deadly.

Dart and the girl had finished their silent communication. As he struggled into his harness, he looked fixedly at me.

"Did you take in what I said? You see the sort of things that are going on here, Mr. Undersecretary of State Roberts —big things. Bigger than your bureaucratic mind can encompass. We're changing the future, *I'm* changing the future here on Moreau Island. Things aren't going to be as they have been. There'll be radical differences. Humans don't have to stay that same antique shape. Change shape, you get changes in function, thinking. . . . It's big, all right. . . ."

As he spoke, his face grew uglier, his mouth more set. His eyes evaded mine. He was sweating.

I turned. Heather was there, pointing the gun at me. When someone holds a gun at you, you look first in their eyes, to see if they mean it—and she did—and then at the weapon, to see what sort of mechanism is going to finish you, if it comes to that. She was using the hypodermic gun she had used before. It was a heavy model, obviously well suited to dropping big brutes like George at a moment's notice.

"Sorry, Roberts," she said. "We have trouble enough. You're bona fide, we grant you that, but we don't need you prowling around at this particular time."

"We're shutting you up for a few hours, Mr. Roberts," Dart said.

I stood by the bed, looking from one to the other. Heather was willing enough to let me have it, but she was nervous about missing. She moved in closer.

"Tie him up," Dart ordered, leaning forward. I heard his harness creak.

That presented her with a problem. She did not want to lay the gun aside. She glanced at a long woven Chinese-type belt that hung behind the door. I jumped at her.

Heather's impulses were fast. With one continuous movement she dropped the gun on the bed, swung about, and brought the edge of her hand up toward my windpipe. But I was moving too. Her blow hit me harmlessly under the arm, and I struck her glancingly across the temple with my fist.

Almost simultaneously, I dived for the gun.

Dart was wearing his prosthetic arms. A metal and plastic

hand grasped my wrist and started to squeeze. I doubled up with the pain—Dart's prosthetic limbs were motor-assisted. When the pressure relaxed, the gun was back with Heather, and she lashed my wrists expertly together. She had avoided the full force of my blow.

"Good girl," Dart said. "Not really hurt, are we? You must get me into the chair and we'll go and see what has to be done in the lab. Let's hope Da Silva is managing."

"Do we leave Roberts behind?" Her voice was perfectly calm.

"Certainly not! He comes with us, where we can keep an eye on him. Roberts, I'm genuinely sorry about this, but you've been a bloody pain in the neck if ever I saw one, and we are not going to let you go back to Washington to make trouble."

"You dirty little amputee, you'd better let me loose or you'll be in even deeper trouble. You know that helicopter is on its way, and it certainly won't leave without me, even if they have to put you in cold storage first!"

As Heather shifted him tenderly off the bed into his wheel-chair, he said—looking not at me, but at some distant corner of the room—"*We're* going to put *you* in cold storage, Roberts. I'll remind you of something you should already know; now you can apply it to the present situation. Hatreds between nations are nothing to interdepartmental hatreds. We're going to put you in cold storage for the duration!"

He had a digital clock by his bed. "Better hurry," I said. "Your rule here lasts precisely five and three-quarter more hours."

But he had me worried. I didn't know what he meant. And I didn't like the way they walked me out of the room, round the corner, and through the other entrance into that accursed lab.

Da Silva was working with an air of silent complaint, slowly mopping up the bloodstains with an electric floor washer. He had already removed the corpses of the dead SRSRs—I suppose I must call them that—as well as Bella's corpse.

The surviving SRSRs, male and female, stood about silently, watching him. They made no attempt to escape from the lab; nor did they make any of the half-fawning, half-threatening obeisances at the entrance of the Master that the Beast People would have done. They looked at him somewhat coldly, and one of the women said, with her perfect diction and uninflected voice, "Bella didn't do you as much harm as we were led to believe."

"Harm enough," he said, patting his turban.

"The Master will probably be permanently blind in one eye," Heather said, addressing herself mainly to the female. "He needs loving care."

"He will have to make do with you," she replied, witheringly.

"Er—well, we shall survive," Dart said. "Sorry for all the trouble. This isn't a fun-fair, you know."

The female SRSR said, "You have a diminished sense of responsibility if that is all you have to say. Eleven of us have been killed, including 415, who was pregnant, as you are well aware. We have all been frightened. As far as we can establish, it was purely through your carelessness that Bella broke in here. We had already warned you about her potential danger and told you to get rid of her."

I could see how uncomfortable Dart was under this peremptory tone, and it was Heather who answered sharply, "We hear too many of your complaints, 402. You know how short of staff we are here. Why don't you do something for a change? Why aren't you helping Da Silva to clear up?"

"We were not responsible for the mess in the first place."

"Through into the Examination Room, the lot of you," Dart said. "I wish to give you all an examination, besides the normal blood check."

At this they protested strongly, but they went, and Heather followed behind Dart's chair, keeping her dark eye on me. When we were all in the Examination Room, which was a glorified surgery, extensively equipped, she shut the door behind us.

The gnome she had referred to as 402 looked up at me and said, "What's this human doing here? Is he on the Program? If so, I don't recognize him. I desire to be better informed concerning him."

"If he was on the Program, he wouldn't be tied up," Dart said. "He is captive, and we're keeping our eye on him till the sub arrives later. Then we ship him out of here."

He put his head down as he spoke; I could not see his facial expression.

"If he's not on the Program, then we are not being examined with him in the room," 402 was saying, gazing at me with fishy distaste. "It's written into our Charter, and we haven't forgotten the fight we had to establish that."

The argument went on, but I lost track of it. The Master, ruffled by the sharp tongues of his SRSRs, had let slip a word not exactly intended for my ears. The supply submarine!

In the general brouhaha, I had forgotten about the sub and the imminence of its visit. They were planning to put me on it as their captive, and presumably it was due to arrive soon. Since they knew that the helicopter would be here by midnight, could it be they expected the sub before that? It seemed likely. Otherwise, they could have thrown me into that cell again and forgotten about me while attending to more urgent matters.

I was aware that to be delivered captive to the submarine commander would put me out of action for some while. That was what Dart meant by his remark, "Hatreds between nations are nothing to interdepartmental hatreds." Once the U.S. Navy had me (and Dart would get me properly signed for to clear himself with the officer i/c of the Search-Rescue helicopter), they would be reluctant to relinquish me to the State Department, and months of obfuscation could pass before I was cleared. Months or years. Certainly long enough for Dart to lodge other complaints against me and render any move against him invalid.

Once I was on the sub, my cause was lost.

The SRSRs took a firm stand on my presence in the room.

"Oh, very well, if you insist on being difficult," Dart said. "Heather, take Roberts right through to the animal pens at the far end and lock him in there, will you? Leave him tied up."

"Okay," she said. "Although I think you give in to these project people far too readily."

Taking me by the arm in cordial fashion, she led me further into the lab complex. The lights were off here, but I could see that planning had been on a generous scale. Scathingly though Dart had spoken of experimental animals, like mice and guinea pigs, there were plenty of them here, sitting in their cages. A monkey chittered at us as we passed, reaching out a hand in appeal.

"You really are a slave to our crippled friend," I said. "You work for him, cook for him, strip for him—what else do you do?"

"The lot," she said. "I was trained for this job and I take pride in doing it well. And I'll take pride in kicking you in the balls if you try anything with me again." She gave me a hard scowling look.

"You must get a great buzz out of the SRSRs! You're going to have to cook and clean for them, and scrape out the bottom of their cage, now that Bella's dead."

"I hate the little bastards, if you must know. But they happen to be part of my job. As for that submarine—mention of which made you prick up your ears so eagerly —we applied for more staff and guards long ago, and they will be aboard this trip. Worry about yourself, not me. I can look after myself."

"And sexy with it," I said, as she locked me in.

"A hell of a lot you care about that!"

Heather held up the key for my inspection, slipped it in a pocket of her tunic, and walked off, buttocks jolting.

I was left in a small bare cell, one of six adjoining each other. The cells were constructed of fifty-millimeter-thick metal rods. They were veritable cages, with bars front, back, and sides, and top and bottom. They had been secured in place by massive bolts bonded into the concrete floor. It was possible for a jailer to walk round the back of the cages and fill the troughs there provided for water and food. My troughs were empty, although old caked meal still lined one of them.

The smell of the place told me that this was where the Beast People were penned while Dart was working on them.

So much I saw before Heather had reached the other end of the chamber. She closed the door behind her as she went, leaving me in gloom. The only windows were overhead, in the roof. I could see blue sky through them, and a scrap of foliage. The only artificial light came from a machine glowing and ticking to itself some meters from where I stood.

A kind of despair enters a man's mind when he finds himself caged. All my muscles locked: my autonomous nervous system was refusing to transmit an impulse to check out the fact that I was in a cage from which I could not escape.

As I stood, gripping the bars, breathing dim fetid air, sounds came to me, music, which at first I could not identify. The music was no louder than a whisper; in sending my hearing out to chase it, rigidity left me. The whisper seemed to tell me that somewhere, if only in theory, happier things existed than the series of degradations I had encountered.

Despite my predicament, that hopeful music brought a kind of enchantment. Then I recognized what it was. It was

Haydn, Haydn again, and his confounded *Clock Symphony*. Not Haydn, but a tape of Haydn projected automatically through the lab complex. No one was listening, not Dart, not Bella, not Heather, not some postoperative ape learning to manipulate a lion's legs. That civilized innocent Haydn had no right to speak to any of us who suffered at the end of this darkening century.

By calling aloud, I tried to din out the insubstantial music. The old Viennese court was dead, and with it all the tidy resolutions contained in its harmonies. On the island it was an obscene anachronism. For a while, I was in a frenzy of senseless activity, out of my mind. When I recovered myself, the symphony was still playing, almost subliminally.

I began to seek about for some protruding object on which I could attempt to loosen or cut my bonds; but the cage makers had taken care of that sort of ambition long ago.

I stood still and thought about praying. But that complex matter was something I would have to sort out with myself later. Right now, I was frantic with anger and the need to escape. I tried to rock the cages; they all gave a few millimeters, after having no doubt been rocked in unison by tormented creatures, but the hope of uprooting them was a vain one. I shook the door; it rattled but did not budge. I stood on the wooden shelf seat; from there I could bang my skull on the bars overhead. There was nothing effective I could achieve.

There was little I could do but stand there and let time pass. With some contortion, I could see the dial of my watch. It was 1835. Maybe five hours before the chopper got here. It would soon be sunset.

Uncharted tracts of time floated by. The air thickened, the light waned. Night was coming. And the submarine.

As I remained there raging, fixing my eyes in useless hope on every object in view—if only I could reach that stepladder, if only I was nearer that lathe—a shuffling noise caught my attention. I could hear the faint movements of the caged animals at the other end of the room; this was different, and closer.

The lab was built of prefabricated metal sections, bolted into place. At this end of the lab, which faced toward the southeast of the island, the roof sloped downward, until it met the end wall behind me no more than two meters above the floor. In this sloping section was the skylight through which I could see the leafed extremity of the branch of a tree and the darkening sky. Someone was up on the roof.

In a moment, a face appeared at the glass.

I could make out only a blurred outline of a head and a sharp muzzle.

Although the Beast People were not great friends, in this emergency anyone was an ally. Whatever they were about up there, they were against Dart, and so on my side. My fear was that, in the gloom of the laboratory, I would not be seen.

Bending backward, I pulled off one of my shoes and struck at the bars with it repeatedly, making as much noise as I could.

The head withdrew from the window. It was replaced a moment later by two heads. I stopped banging and waggled my leg through the bars at them, relying on the sharpness of their eyes. And in any case, I realized, they might well be looking to see if any of their kind was imprisoned, knowing the cages of old.

They had seen me! One of them—now I was almost sure it was Bernie—raised a pole and drove it down on the glass. The glass shattered and came tinkling down to the floor. It was reinforced, but the pair of them struck at the wire core ferociously and broke it down. I dared not call encouragement lest, finding who it was, they left me there.

The wire mesh fell away. One of the two figures jumped down and landed lightly on all fours, just beyond my cage.

"Bernie!" I said. "It's Roberts—your friend, remember me? Good boy, well done!"

"Good boy, good man, hero, yes. Big stuff! No trouble."

He sidled up to the bars. I caught the blank red gleam of his eyes in the gathering dark.

"Get me out of here, Bernie. Open the cage, break it open, find a strong bar if you can."

He rattled the bars. "No key, gone Master. You keep in cage like sad beast."

"Get me out! Find a bar, fetch it, good boy!"

He went off vaguely, searching and sniffling. The monkeys started up a great chatter, throwing themselves about their cages, and I was afraid that Heather or Dart would come in. But Bernie returned after a while with a great flat bar with ratchets along one side.

We inserted it between door and doorway, just above the lock, and threw our weight on it. The teeth grated and gripped, the chilled steel seemed to give a little. Over and over, we leaned all our weight against it. Gradually, the lock yielded under the combined pressure. One last heave, and it clicked open. I staggered out of the cage.

Bernie spent a while fumbling with his malformed hands at the strap that bound me. Finally, it fell to the floor. I clasped his shoulder.

"Very good boy, my friend," I said.

"You here bad place, my friend hero. Soon Foxy Man take flame, you Foxy Man, he take flame, flame up all Master. Bad place go soon. Lab'raty go Big Sky."

"Great! Let's get out of here," I said. "The sooner the better." Slipping on my shoe, I ran for the stepladder I had previously glared at with such envy and set it up under the broken window. I went first, climbing out on the roof, helping Bernie up after me.

It was a shock to find that his companion on the roof was one of the ape-men—whether Alpha or Beta, whether the one I had grappled with on Warren's roof or not, I could not tell, although it struck me that I should try to avoid roofs in future. He came toward me, but after a few muttered words of explanation from Bernie, he slunk back and contented himself with glaring at me and making faces involving displays of sharp teeth.

Outside, it was less dark than I had imagined. It was just past 1900. I saw how the Beasts had gained access to the roof. A long rope had been tied high in a tree to one side of the buildings; the other end had then been taken round to a tree on the other side, and secured at an equal height. It was then simple enough to climb out along the rope over the high fence and drop down, although they could hardly have carried out the plan if the inhabitants of the HQ had not been otherwise occupied.

Even so, it was an ambitious plan. I knew who was behind it before I saw him. There was an impatient yip from the bushes behind us, Bernie answered in kind, and Foxy could be discerned, prowling on the other side of the barrier. I could make out other shapes, other eyes, behind him; the Beast People were gathered in strength. Foxy was carrying a light of some kind.

He called to me, "Hey, hero, what you do? You no Beast People. I still got the shoot-gun. I now easy shoot you."

"I'm coming down. I'm getting away from the Master. He's no friend of mine. You can see for yourself, the Master dumped me in the same lockup he used on you."

"You come down fast."

I was glad to get down. It was easy enough to work my way across the rope and slide down the tree to the ground. Foxy was waiting tensely for me at the bottom. He carried an old army dixie; in it, a little fire of twigs burned. As I came close, he set the dixie down and unslung a carbine from round his shoulders. He held it at the ready, pointing toward my feet.

"Fire!" he said proudly, indicating the dixie with a bushy red eyebrow. He had overcome one of the basic animal fears.

Curiously, I stared at him, the creature who had tried to kill me. He looked like a real brigand. He still wore his tattered cloak while on his head was that symbol of authority, George's old leather hat.

He tapped his prow-shaped chest. "Foxy me you no longer more afraid flame like all Beast People. Me shoot shoot-gun, kill George, kill anybody people, you savvy, hero? Me man same you, use flame, savvy?"

"I savvy only too well."

"Good savvy well. Me same you, me shoot-gun you killed, you give trouble, hero." A skein of saliva ran down silver from his jaw as he looked me over to estimate the effect of his threats. "Now is all time finish." He knew he had not got right what he wanted to say, and so repeated it, still regarding me slyly. "Now is time all finish. Master go. We you Beast People get up burn Master Death Place Lab'raty down, Master kill with shoot-gun, savvy? . . ."

It was a long speech. More saliva ran to the ground like quicksilver. Then he added emphatically, "We be this place Master, all Master."

Malformed and hostile faces peered at me. The flame flickering in the dixie illuminated fangs as well as eyeballs. I did not intend to challenge them.

"You'll never set fire to this place with that small light. Listen, get a big branch burning well. Climb right to the far end of the HQ. Look down into the compound, savvy? Many paint pots there, belong to dead Hans. Paint burns fast and well. Best idea. Drop the burning branch on paint pots."

His red gaze bored at mine.

He gave one nod of his head. As he turned away to get the others moving, he said slyly, "You savvy I get this flame where from you friends on Seal Rock. Lorta, she give me flame in tin when I give her rum and bully tinmeat. You like

Lorta. I savvy." Solemnly, he tapped his head, then his genitals. His gesture was more companionable than contemptuous; he had placed me now.

Then he turned to drive the other Beast People forward and get the plan into action. They pressed past me, conspiratorial, no longer nervous of my presence, grotesque of eye and facial form and body, yet no longer one half as alien to me as once they had been. They had moved closer to man. I had moved closer to them.

Standing there in the dark before slipping away, seeing them press past, I recalled how the fable of H. G. Wells, when the beasts on his island had slowly degenerated from the human back to the animal, sounded a note of melancholy. These actual beasts were slowly advancing from the animal to the human; and I could not find it in my heart to think that less melancholy.

It was now entirely dark. I was at a disadvantage among the trees. Foxy had gone to join the ape-man and Bernie on the roof; I could hear Bernie whimpering his approval of Foxy's presence—poor Bernie had found a new master to follow. The other animals were advancing stealthily forward along the stockade, keeping pace with those above them. I was free to go; I had interfered enough; what happened now must be played out without intervention from me.

The time was moving toward 1930. In four or five hours, the helicopter from Fiji should be here. And the submarine?

My safest plan was to remain somewhere out of harm's way. In the dark, I could not get very far. I regretted having neither torch nor gun with me. I wondered about Heather. Dart and the saturnine Da Silva must accept whatever fate befell them; for Heather, I could not put away a sneaking sympathy.

I would wait by the mouth of the lagoon. The submarine would arrive there, but I could hide away above it on the eastern side of the mouth where the cliff began to rise. From there, I could also keep a watch toward the HQ.

The moon, now on the wane, was already shining, although it provided little light. I moved slowly toward the water, half reluctant to leave the vicinity of the HQ. As I went, a flame leaped up somewhere behind me.

Foxy's simple stratagem was working. The paint was dope- rather than lead-based, and highly inflammable. The flame spread among Maastricht's old discarded cans, rising and setting fire to the branches of trees standing just inside the compound. A great light spread and continued to grow. The fascination of all fires is such that I turned to watch. I doubted whether the blaze was going to be enough to catch the HQ itself alight.

The brilliance of the flames enabled me to see the figure of Foxy, dancing on the roof. At the same time, savage shouts came to my ears, and a group of Beast People charged at the gate of the compound. They carried a battering ram. It struck the gate with force. They pulled back and struck a second time.

Before they could strike a third time, a new light was turned on the scene.

This was a colder and more powerful light. Roughly circular in shape, it blazed somewhere along to my right, in the woods above the village, and slid rapidly along until it transfixed the invaders at the gate. In dismay, they stopped still and turned to glare into the searchlight.

Belatedly, I dropped flat. The submarine had arrived. The beam was shining from its conning tower. The time was 1935.

The waters of the lagoon were no more than sixty meters from me. Squinting toward the source of the light, I estimated that the vessel was about as far from the shore. I could hear the voices of the crew. They spoke English. So Dart's allies had arrived. He was probably in radio contact with them.

Only for a moment were the Beast People transfixed by the light. Then they broke ranks and dashed away in all directions into the darkness.

A machinegun opened up on the submarine. They had left it a bit too late, but I saw one of the sullen Bull Men hit. He made a leap into the air, fell clumsily, rolled over, and lay there twitching.

Finding myself uncomfortably near the line of fire, I crawled into the undergrowth. It was as well I did, because the searchlight now began swinging from side to side, the machinegun chattering at random. A heavy goat shape blundered past me, fell into a bush, and forged on through the undergrowth, croaking in terror. Under this new threat, the Beast People were as much of a menace as they had ever been.

It was best to keep to my plan and make for the cliff by the lagoon mouth. I moved forward again, keeping as low as possible. The firing stopped in a moment, presumably because there were no more moving targets to fire at; but I was too busy looking after myself to keep account of what was going on elsewhere. Now and again, I heard the sound of bodies pushing frantically through the undergrowth.

I was gasping as I climbed the last few meters and hauled myself up to a rocky ledge. There I could sprawl, half concealed by bushes from the action in the center of the island. For a while, I simply lay like a dog, desperately trying to recover my breath.

When I looked again, I saw how greatly the fire about the HQ had spread. Whole trees were burning like torches. I fancied that the HQ itself was now on fire.

The submarine was in clear view; the reflection of the fire in the water threw part of it into silhouette. A dinghy had been launched and was now at the quayside, where a party of twelve marines and an officer were smartly disembarking and forming up. The searchlight, meanwhile, was circling slowly about the surrounding parts of the island. When it came near me, I hugged the ground. Now and again, the machinegun spoke. Some poor creature was screaming away in the bushes.

Thinking I would be safer with a little rock between me and the arena, I waited until the light had gone by again, then climbed hastily to the top of the rock, sprawling at full length and feeling down over the dark side for a possible ledge. Otherwise, there would be just a precipitous slope between me and the ocean; the waves were breaking only a meter and a half below me—I could feel their spray on my arm and face.

The nearest thing to a ledge was a buttress of rock, upon the sloping top of which I could crouch for a short spell at least and feel myself safe, while being able to watch what went on.

Heaving myself cautiously over the lip of rock, I saw a light out to sea. I was too afraid of falling onto rocks and getting myself drowned to pay attention to it until I was wedged on my pitiable bit of buttress.

Then I saw that Moreau Island had an answering fire on its satellite. The cover of Seal Island was blazing furiously. Through the smoke pall that hung low over the intervening waters, I saw the palms spring suddenly into flame!

My heart went out to Lorta and the laughing men and little Satsu. My imagination only too readily traced a likely cause for the catastrophe. I had given them the gift of fire. They had built their own fires and traded the gift for—Foxy's phrase came back to me—for rum and bully tinmeat. How eagerly their sportive natures would take to drunkenness! And in that drunken orgy, they had set fire to their crude shelter, and had probably perished in the blaze. I gazed and gazed in stricken remorse across the dark water.

Here was another aspect of the process in which I had played a fatal part. . . .

Crouching there in defeated state, I scarcely took in the shouting coming from the direction of the lagoon. I needed no more data on the world. Nevertheless, being human, I finally raised my head above the level of the rock against which I crouched and looked in at the violent island once more.

More marines were ashore. One party had marched round to search the native village. Whether inadvertently or according to instructions, they had set it on fire, so that yet another destructive beacon lit the night.

The HQ was now well alight. The senior blaze was also the biggest. Sparks rose high into the tropical air, whirling upward in a short-lived dance toward the stars. A party of marines was drawn up outside the stockades—well clear, I noted, of the upright George, who remained motionless at his post throughout the proceedings.

The marines were on escort duty, and the reason for their presence had just appeared. In good order, Mortimer Dart and his company were leaving the doomed building. The light from the fires was so bright that I could make out individual figures clearly.

First came Heather, escorting the SRSRs. Both she and they walked forward with no sign of panic that I could discern, although this was very likely the first time the subrace had ever left their laboratory. Heather carried bags or cases in each hand.

Behind her and her flock came Da Silva, pushing a large trolley loaded with metal boxes. No doubt Dart's precious records and formulas were there. Last, following Da Silva, came Dart himself.

It occurred to me to wonder why they had been so long leaving the building—not because they had stopped to release all the helpless experimental animals. Dart must have had a more practical reason—or perhaps it was just that he had at first refused to believe that his citadel was going up in smoke.

In all events, he was leaving with a brave show. He had climbed into his cyborg suit, and now began to stump toward the submarine as I had first seen him, more a massive robot than a man.

As the party came forward, a marine was running and gesticulating. The escort raised their short-snouted rifles.

On the roof of the burning building—a figure, also armed! I knew who it was, even as I marveled that he had not fled or else perished from the heat. But perhaps the angle of the roof shielded him from the worst of it.

He took careful aim, bemused by the smoke. The marines opened fire on him.

Everyone else started running. Then Foxy fired his shot.

The gigantic robot lurched. He stood still, then twisted sideways, then collapsed.

My glance sped back to the roof. Of Foxy there was no longer any sign. A cloud of smoke obscured everything. It was 2010.

A marine officer was shouting through a bull-roarer, his voice audible above the roar of burning.

"Okay, you guys, get to him. Ma'am, will you and your party keep walking this way please. Straight into the dinghy before there's more trouble. We'll take care of Dr. Dart."

The marines lifted Dart gently out of his harness: from the giant came forth a small child. It seemed that he might be alive still; I could not tell. He was carried into the boat, and to the submarine, which had already devoured Heather and the rest of his party, including his patent invention, the gnome-like subrace.

The last section of marines was returning smartly from its patrol. One final shot was fired into the shadows. Then those men too were swallowed into the black shape in the lagoon.

No moving figure, however remotely human, was left. The fires blazed on an empty scene. Fire and darkness, fire and darkness—the elements of the human psyche. . . .

A voice near me said, "Calvary, you are you yourself, is it?"

As if in a dream, I looked down to seaward, to the figures scrambling over the surges toward me.

"Lorta, is that you?"

"My funny Calvy, yes! Who else am I? We swim to see you, all, all here."

"Satsu?"

"Me here, Calvy! Your little sucky Satsu."

Leaning over, I extended an arm, and the others helped the girl up to me. Since it now appeared safe to emerge above my ridge, I guided them over one by one. Even at that hour, they laughed and chuckled, swearing that I tickled them where I had no right to do while others were about. Soon we were huddled together on a safe ledge.

"Soon I am going to take you all with me to another place," I said.

"That's so good," one of the men said. "Is it a better place?"

"Another place. Not exactly better . . . more to eat, at least. . . ." I could say no more.

The submarine was moving. So silent were its motors that we heard nothing but the clip of the waves. It slipped away, over the lip of the lagoon into the deep waters, and was gone, and all its dangerous knowledge with it, heading for a world that thought it needed such knowledge.

The fires seemed less brilliant. Certainly the blaze over at the village was almost dead, the other blazes dying.

A figure limped out of the bush and down toward the water's edge. It wandered near the spot where Maastricht had drowned, many a long day ago. It set up a howl of desolation, like a lost dog.

Holding tightly to Satsu, I looked at my watch.

The time was 2055.

As usual, it was a matter of waiting. Of sitting tight and waiting.

The light died until the night itself had almost a material quality, like a body of which the still glowing remains of Dart's headquarters represented a wound. In due time, the sullen crimson of the wound lit the belly of a helicopter.

The machine sank lower. It surveyed the land by infrared. The downward pressure of wind from its vanes created a pattern on the margins of the sea, veining it in a half circle until the beaten water resembled a hastily discarded shawl. This illusion vanished as the machine landed and cut its engines. The waves resumed their usual pounding of the rocks.

Some shadowy figures were collected from the beach of Moreau Island, after which the vanes of the machine recommenced to turn. The helicopter lifted, and again was caught briefly in the glow of dying fires before it vanished into the night.

On the forsaken island, a solitary figure, part man, part dog, emerged from its place of concealment and scuttled toward the edge of the sea. Time and again it ran into the waves, howling, only to run howling back again, finally to stand in bafflement on the rocks, staring out over the Pacific, as if attempting to resolve a riddle it could barely formulate.

Beneath the surface of the ocean, night and day were less distinct events than on the rest of the planet. The creatures of land were governed by the absence or presence of direct sunlight; below the waves, a different set of factors obtained. On the ocean bed, a permanent twilight reigned but, even on its upper levels, the water permitted its denizens to continue their activities with general indifference to the time of day.

A philosophical observer might see here an analogy with the human brain, between the parts labeled, for convenience if not accuracy, conscious and unconscious. The conscious brain is accustomed to a regular series of waking and sleeping states which correspond to light and dark. Matters are less clear-cut in the unconscious; a different set of clocks ticks. The unconscious has its own submarine element, unpunctuated by sun. The difference is between Reason, which invented the twenty-four-hour clock, and Instinct, which keeps to its own Great Time. Until humanity comes to an armistice between these yin–yang factors, there is no armistice possible on Earth. The bombs will fall.

The bombs fell. The great ocean contained many peripheral seas: the Guatemala Basin, the Tasman Sea, the Coral Sea, the South China Sea, the Yellow Sea, the Sea of Japan, the Sea of Okhotsk, the Bering Sea. Over all these seas, conflict flared as ideologies clashed and nation warred with nation.

Debris from various combats fell into the ocean, sank, disappeared into oozes far below the surface. Devastatingly effective products of chemical warfare rained down. The ocean absorbed them all. The ocean covered a third of the globe; it was in a sense the mother element of the globe; and could survive most of the activities of its brood. But the day would come when it could absorb no more. Then it would die, and the planet with it.

The question was whether humanity's instinct for survival would impel it to find a way to permanent peace. Otherwise, all would be lost. For the ocean was ultimately no more enduring than Instinct alone, or unaided Reason.

ABOUT THE AUTHOR

Brian Aldiss' first book was a semi-autobiographical piece called *The Brightfount Diaries* about a young man working for a bookseller, but his major publications have been in the science fiction field, starting with the short stories collected in *Space, Time and Nathaniel* (published in the U.S. as *No Time Like Tomorrow*) and continuing through his Hugo Award–winning *Hothouse* to his more recent successes with *Frankenstein Unbound* and *The Malacia Tapestry*.

He was for many years the book reviewer for *The Oxford Mail* and has published the standard history of science fiction, *Billion Year Spree*. Recently he has edited a series of anthologies covering many of the most famous themes in science fiction *(Galactic Empires, Space Odysseys)*.

Aldiss, who has been regarded as a major literary figure in England for a number of years, has had several popular successes throughout the 1970s with his series of novels covering the growth and sexual experiences of Horatio Stubbs *(The Hand-Reared Boy, A Soldier Erect, A Rude Awakening)*.

He lives with his wife and children in a small town outside Oxford and travels extensively.